A Quiet
Little Killing

He opened the door in the swimming-bath enclosure and went inside. The pool, lying in a hollow, was in shadow and he walked downward into twilight as he descended the steps leading to the small wooden pavilion which served as a storage place for much of the groundsman's equipment.

He did not hear the soft footstep behind him, and he was barely aware of any pain. But he felt the jug slip from his fingers on to the pavement and through strangely blurred vision he saw the dark water coming up to meet him.

Killing No Murder

Howard Shaw

PINNACLE BOOKS   NEW YORK

KILLING NO MURDER

Copyright © 1972 by Colin Howard

A Pinnacle Books edition, published by special arrangement with Charles Scribner's Sons.

First printing June/1984

ISBN: 0-523-41785-3

Can. ISBN: 0-523-43200-3

Cover art by Dan Wagner

Printed in the United States of America

PINNACLE BOOKS, INC.
1430 Broadway
New York, New York 10018

9 8 7 6 5 4 3 2 1

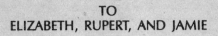

TO
ELIZABETH, RUPERT, AND JAMIE

Killing No Murder was the title of a pamphlet, published in 1657 and usually ascribed to the Leveller Edward Sexby, suggesting that Oliver Cromwell should die for the good of the country.

KILLING
NO MURDER

CHAPTER ONE

PADDINGTON STATION has many guises: to holidaying hordes, armed with the *Daily Mirror* and chocolate-covered children, it is the springboard for a wet week in Torquay or Paignton; to country dwellers up for a day's shopping in the West End it is in the morning the first glimpse of the seething metropolis, in the evening a haven of peace where parcels can be put down and feet rested; to myriads of schoolboys it represents the beginning and end of the holidays. Here, at the end of each term, carriage loads of multi-colored-capped boys are returned, scrubbed and semi-educated, to their rightful owners; here the same boys congregate before being dispatched to the wilds of the West Country by suddenly light-hearted parents. For the boys it is a station of two moods: paradise and purgatory. It is with the downward movement of this inexorable cycle of hope and despair that our story opens.

" 'Ere y'are, mate. Where's yer dad?" Porter Guffin gave the last of three heavy suitcases a decisive shove into the compartment, tipped his cap to the back of his head, and

1

looked around for the father who might reward the assistance rendered to a son.

The son, Browning, a slow-witted boy just about to embark on his third term at Claydon Court Preparatory School, grimaced, peered myopically down the platform and said "I don't know" in a tone of voice which implied that he did not greatly care.

Guffin grunted somewhere at the back of his throat, produced a cigarette stub, and stood back with his hands on his hips. He did not mind waiting.

Browning had lost interest in the porter by now and had started a detailed examination of the ash-tray next to his seat. His fingers were already a dirty gray color and he evinced interest in the remains of a screwed-up chocolate wrapping.

Two boys appeared in the corridor.

"Oh, no! Look who's here!"

"We'll soon kick him out."

Browning looked up as the sliding door opened. His defensive expression showed clearly that he had overheard the threat to eject him. "Hullo," he said.

"You can't stay here, Browning. We've bagged the whole compartment. What have you done with the cricket bat that was on that seat?" The taller of the two newcomers opened the attack.

"I—Oh—It's on the floor. Are you sure there's no room? I couldn't find a place anywhere else."

"Hard luck. You'll have to stand in the corridor. All these seats are bagged—and even if they weren't, there wouldn't be room for you."

The conversation followed the usual schoolboy lines. Browning, at least six months younger than Best and Keyworth and therefore very much nearer the bottom of the school hierarchy, removed himself to the corridor where he was soon joined by his luggage, unceremoniously bundled out behind him.

Patterns such as this were worked out in many of the compartments reserved for the school. Popular boys had their presence courted by several compartments; others, the outcasts, were spurned everywhere and drifted into little groups formed by others of their kind. Around them, looking embarrassed and overdressed, stood parents of all shapes and sizes.

John Warren, Second Master at Claydon Court, glanced at his watch and checked it with the station clock. They agreed: 12:25; five minutes to go. Just time to go round the school compartments to try to fit unwanted boys into seats and to make sure that the natural high spirits of the beginning of term were being contained. Warren was well aware that the boys considered the train a sort of no-man's land between parental control and school discipline and had every intention of seeing that the interregnum was firmly handled; indeed, he was equally well aware that he was one of the few members of staff capable of dealing with this particular problem.

Warren was in his early fifties but looked younger. Slim and upright, as yet he gave no hint of the heaviness that so often comes in middle age to athletic men. His face, square-set and dominated by sandy eyebrows, was of that ageless type which is firmly molded at twenty-one and matures only imperceptibly. A faint recession of the hair and wrinkles by the eyes were the only indications of his true age.

His first port of call was an empty compartment he was keeping for himself. Warren had fixed ideas on the correct relationship between masters and boys and believes there should be a gulf of mutual respect between them. He had been a captain in the Gunners during the war and now treated the boys rather as if they were 'other ranks.' On this occasion he had no intention of traveling down to Claydon wedged in with boys and shrewdly judged they would be happier without him.

His private compartment remained empty. A tough-looking little boy stood at the door, a self-appointed guard. "It's all right, sir. I'll see no one gets in here."

"Well done, Clarkson. Have you got a seat for yourself?"

"Yes, thank you, sir. I was one of the first here and—er—I managed to get a good seat."

"I'll bet you did," was Warren's unspoken tribute. From odd snippets of conversation he had overheard, he gathered that Clarkson had bagged five compartments and then sublet them to later arrivals for an unspecified rent. A clever boy, he thought, and was just turning away from the door when a hand was placed on his shoulder.

"Hullo, John. Would you like a bit of assistance with the mob?"

Warren turned and came face to face with Mark Begbie, a colleague at the school who taught French and helped him run the games. "Hullo, Mark. What are you doing here? Aren't you driving down?"

"No. I've sold my motor-car. Aren't you pleased to see me?"

Warren smiled at the correctness of 'my motor-car,' and with genuine pleasure. He was delighted he had someone to share the peace of his private compartment and also looked forward to a distribution of the police duties. Of all the staff at Claydon, Begbie was the one for whom he had most time; and that was saying something.

"Put your luggage in here. We'll have this one to ourselves. I'll just go and make sure everyone's accounted for. I nearly left Randall-Jones behind last time. His mother was very hurt—she thought we didn't want him."

Begbie, only just twenty-six, climbed into the carriage and swung a decrepit suitcase deftly on to the rack. He was a lean young man, almost gangling, with sensitive features and an unruly lock of auburn hair that he was constantly and ineffectually sweeping back. He stuck his head out of the window, then thought better of it and hurriedly withdrew when he saw the large numbers of parents who might buttonhole him at any moment.

"Close shave," he breathed, and fell back into the corner seat with his back to the direction of danger. He had been at Claydon for two years now, but had still not accustomed himself to producing the pious platitudes required by parents who found the truth unpalatable and insisted against all the evidence on viewing their progeny through rose-tinted spectacles. It was one of the few things that made him angry.

This was odd, for Begbie was not usually irate about anything. Indeed, a capacity for ambling through life without ever being unduly disturbed was his distinguishing characteristic. At Oxford he had done little work, played a great deal of rugger and cricket, and taken a poor Third. Faced with the necessity of earning his living, he had been forced to choose between industry, for which he had no inclination, and an academic life, for which the examiners had given him little qualification. At the eleventh hour—literally, for he had been about to accept a lowly post with a firm making plastic bottles for detergents—that same uncle who had pulled strings to get him into B.N.C. once more cleared the debris from the ill-defined path of his future career. He had found himself selected for the French post at Claydon by a headmaster who, retiring at the end of the year, removed some tiresome deskwork by appointing the first applicant to present himself for interview.

The train started. Begbie stopped musing about the

shortcomings of parents and noted that with the shrilling of the guard's whistle another term had begun. Events were to take an unpleasant course before a similar whistle at the tiny village station of Claydon Prior announced that it had ended.

CHAPTER TWO

THE train gathered speed past tenements, gas-works, coal-tips, and the other bric-à-brac which cluster near London termini. With Claydon Prior a good two and a half hours away the boys settled down to play games, read or talk. Warren returned from his tour of inspection and sat down in the corner opposite Begbie.

"There don't seem to be any riots so far. Did you have a good holiday, Mark?"

"Yes, thanks. I haven't done much, but it's been peaceful. A concert or two, some rugger, and a spot of fishing. How about you?"

"I had a week with an old army friend of mine in Scotland and we did some walking, but I haven't done anything wildly exciting either."

Considering that the two men usually got on well together, this opening attempt at conversation was not very successful. They looked out of the window at the advertisements littering the sides of the line and the sprawling suburbia of Ealing and Southall. Now that they were running free of London's perpetual pall of grime it could be seen that the sky was blue; a warm sun threatened to make it the first day of summer.

Begbie glanced at Warren out of the corner of his eye. As he thought, Warren was staring out of the window but his mind was quite definitely on something else. His eyes were fixed and unfocused; the corners of his mouth turned down; the lines at the sides of his eyes were creased with concentration. Then the eyes flickered back to the present as the train lumbered over an untidy set of points. Begbie turned his attention back to the washing hanging in the pathetic back gardens near the line until he in his turn found himself gazing unseeingly out of the window and felt a thick depression envelop him. Then, suddenly, he knew why Warren was being so unsociable; he knew why they were having difficulty in mustering ammunition for a reasonable conversation. They were both preoccupied with the prospect of another term at Claydon under the new Headmaster.

Now that both men realized that they were meditating on the same topic, it became a bridge between them as effective as it had been a barrier only seconds before. "How's the pious principal?" enquired Begbie facetiously.

Warren looked at his feet before answering. The progressive innovations of the new Head had hit him harder than most. "Well, he's still there, I'm afraid." He smiled thinly, then added fiercely: "My God! You'd think he had more sense. He's been here two terms and hasn't learned a single lesson. He just doesn't know the meaning of the word discipline. It's all very well for the university authorities to throw in the sponge and let students do as they like, but these are *children*."

Begbie smiled at the vehemence of this outburst, but there was no response from the older man. His sandy eyebrows rose in surprised arches. "It's all very well for you, Mark, but I've been at Claydon longer than anyone and I'm very unhappy about the school. A year ago it was first class, one of the best prep. schools in the country. Now, thanks to Carter's half-baked ideas, it's going down the drain fast."

There was an element of self-pity in his voice, but Begbie sympathized. "I know how you feel, John. I may not be the world's biggest stickler for discipline, but things were getting bad last term, particularly towards the end."

"I'll be honest, Mark. If there's not a radical improvement soon, I shall leave. I may be a stuffy old reactionary, but I'm not going to stay on while the boys run riot and pull the school down. If Carter wants it, it's going to be hard to stop him, but I'm not going to have anything to do with it."

"Don't be surprised if I join you on the transfer list. I'm no keener on these holy reforms than you are. The thing that worries me most is the appalling manners of the boys. Before Carter came I was quite proud to take the boys out in public, though it sounds silly to say so. Now I dread the thought of taking them anywhere."

The next half hour passed swiftly as the two masters discussed the Head's defects and considered the gloomy prospect of the new term. Soon Reading was passed and the train began its run beside the disused Kennet and Avon canal. Locks fast falling into decay vied with encroaching weeds to create a melancholy impression; yet not an unpleasing one, for there is something inherently attractive about nature reclaiming its own. Begbie was just thinking that the canal matched his own mood and wondering whether it might not have made an excellent subject for a Wordsworth sonnet when Warren interrupted.

"Time for a spot check, I fancy. Just to make sure they're behaving themselves. Coming?"

"I might as well stretch my legs." Begbie stood up,

glanced at his tie in the mirror, unconsciously smoothed down his hair with one hand and followed Warren into the corridor.

The two men made a brief tour of inspection to satisfy themselves that all was peaceful. Boys who noticed them go by waved a friendly greeting. Just when it seemed they might return to their seats, a sudden movement caught Warren's eye.

"Hullo," he said. "Did you see that splash in the canal? Someone's just chucked something out of the window. Come on, I think it came from the next carriage."

He moved swiftly off to investigate and was just in time to see a second missile leave the train. A cheer came from the compartment whence it had been flung, but it died almost immediately as a hoarse voice shouted, "Cave, the Rabbit!"

Warren appeared at the door even as the cheer faded and before the boys could assume attitudes of innocence. As it was, they stood still, their very sheepishness confirming their guilt.

"What was thrown from this window?" demanded Warren, running his eye over his capture. A sense of anger that the boys had dared to flout his authority conflicted with a sense of satisfaction at having caught them.

There was no answer. They boys were not frightened of owning up, but as they were all obviously involved nobody was anxious to precipitate the crisis.

"I'm waiting," said Warren.

This time all the boys tried to speak at once. Warren silenced them with a peremptory hand. "Wheeler-Brown?"

"Well, sir, we were just trying to see who could reach the canal, sir." He pointed out of the window, but the canal was no longer with the train.

"Yes, sir, and I'd just done it," broke in another boy,

obviously proud of his achievement. "No one else had," he added as an afterthought.

"Parkhouse only managed it because he had a bigger bulb," said a third boy, who immediately wished he hadn't, for the others indicted him with their eyes. Authority had been given another clue.

"What sort of bulb, Harris?" Warren demanded, his eyebrows arched in threatening inquiry.

"Well, sir, you see, sir—er—it was like this, sir . . . ." After an uncertain start, Wheeler-Brown launched himself into a lengthy explanation which gathered impetus as his fertile imagination seized on any irrelevancy likely to distract from the central issue.

Warren interrupted the flow: "I asked about the bulbs, Wheeler-Brown."

The boy steeled himself visibly. "Well, sir, actually they were the electric light bulbs from this compartment and the one next door." He plunged on: "You see, sir, we tried them and they didn't work, sir, so we didn't think they would be missed." Five pairs of eyes glanced up at the rounded roof where four empty sockets stared accusingly downwards.

"That's quite enough, Wheeler-Brown. This is sheer vandalism and there can be no possible excuse for it—no excuse at all. I will say no more now, but you will be punished when we reach school. You will all report to me immediately after supper."

Begbie, who had observed the confrontation from the corridor, was impressed by the silence that had fallen over the compartment. He was slightly surprised that Warren had said no more, but rightly judged that he had been rendered more or less speechless by the enormity of the outrage.

The boys sat down as the two masters departed. "What do you think he'll do?" asked one.

"Take us to Carter for a beating," replied Wheeler-

Brown, who was always a realist. "He doesn't hesitate, you know that."

"That'll make a good start to the term," said the boy whose bulb had successfully reached the canal. "I've never been whacked on the first day of term before."

"Bet you Carter doesn't whack," said the boy who had spoken first, a noted optimist. "He hasn't hit anybody yet."

"The Rabbit will be jolly angry if he doesn't. When he sends anybody to the Big Door, he expects him to come back with a sore backside."

"I think Carter's wet," volunteered a boy of limited vocabulary who had not yet spoken. "He talks too much. I wish he would whack somebody."

"This'll give him a good opportunity to start."

"I wish the Rabbit was Head."

"So do I. At least you know where you are. When he says something he means it."

"It's been a rotten year so far."

"I wonder if Carter *will* whack us?"

Back in the peace of their private compartment, Warren and Begbie held a more restrained conversation on the same subject. Carter had told the staff at the beginning of the year that he proposed to run the school without corporal punishment and so far had kept to his plans. He had wisely refrained from telling the boys of his intentions, but after several culprits had returned from the Big Door with unblemished posteriors and surprised smiles it was apparent that the new broom was beginning to sweep.

Opinion amongst the boys was sharply divided. "We're going soft," was the cry of that hardened section of the community which paid regular visits to the place of execution and which resented the removal of a source of bravado. "Bad thing for the juniors," was the verdict of the more responsible seniors, who found the lower half of the school increasingly lacking in respect for those in authority. Some of the frailer brethren—who were never beaten anyway—were genuinely relieved to find a constant threat no longer hanging over them, but many of the boys clearly saw the change as a direct invitation to misbehave.

The staff was united in its hostility to the new order, differing only in degree; but it might have been induced to accept the change if the removal of the cane had not gone hand in hand with a general relaxation of discipline in other directions. The two terms of his headship had seen several crises, including the resignation of a master, a stormy meeting between Carter and Warren, and a staff meeting at which even Begbie had criticized the Head's innovations.

So it was not surprising that the conversation in the two compartments should have centered on the same topic and it was still being discussed when the train stopped at Claydon Prior, high in the Mendip Hills.

On the platform Begbie helped a small bespectacled boy struggling with a trunk of extravagant proportions. "What on earth have you got in here, Wrigley?" he enquired.

"Mostly food, sir. My mother says I must build myself up."

A warm afternoon sun shone down on the platform from a cloudless sky and Begbie felt distinctly uncomfortable in his well-cut tweeds. The sun, too, was to play its part in the events of the term.

CHAPTER THREE

HENRY CARTER had the best intentions. After twenty years spent maturing his ideas at an obscure prep school in Welsh Marches, he had been appointed to the headship of Claydon, where he hoped to put his theories into practice. People who met him once found him mild and affable; those who knew him better discovered an egoistical self-confidence beneath the surface. He was both puritanical and 'progressive,' a curious combination of qualities not as paradoxical as it might appear. As a man of principle, sincere and dedicated, he had swallowed uncritically many of the shallow ideas peddled by educationists whose personal connection with the classroom is usually short and frequently unsuccessful. He certainly believed that the school would be a better place with a relaxation of discipline and no one could say that he did not aim at the happiness of the boys. Unfortunately his personality was not up to the strains his aims placed upon it. His idealism was almost totally unqualified by common sense and he lacked that streak of ruthlessness always essential when change is to be brought to a traditional institution.

His appearance did little to help him. Short and thickset, with a round, almost chubby face, he was in all senses unremarkable. Though only forty-seven, his hair was completely gray, but it failed to lend him any distinction, suggesting rather care and fatigue. He might have done something for himself with well-chosen clothes, but he wore dowdy suits that fitted only where they touched and on one occasion had horrified Begbie by greeting him in his braces, a social solecism the latter found hard to forgive.

On his arrival at the school, nervous, smiling and kindly, the staff had not been displeased by his initial impression. However, one or two heads had shaken when he announced his intentions of abolishing the cane, the doubts were being openly expressed as his second term reached the half-way mark. The boys were slow to take advantage of the loosening of the reins and to some extent were still, psychologically at least, under the discipline of the previous Head. But by the end of term one master had given his notice.

As well as being an idealist, Carter was also an optimist, so he tended to drift from crisis to crisis without realizing that each peak of discontent was slightly higher than the last. Thus, by the beginning of the summer term, with his worries mellowed by four weeks of holiday and his intellect stimulated by a successful piece of historical research, he was hoping for a smooth passage. It was, therefore, with a sense of acute disappointment that he found five boys outside his study door after supper on the very first night.

"Who sent you, Peter?" Calling boys by their Christian names was part of his plan.

Wheeler-Brown, the natural leader of the accused, began his explanations for the second time that day, laying acute emphasis on the uselessness of the bulbs and the fact that nobody had been hurt by the escapade. He had crossed the

Head's path before and he knew the line to take: if possible, he must make Carter think, "Boys will be boys."

When Wheeler-Brown's account had dragged to its conclusion—Carter considered it a bad thing to interrupt—he told the boys to go into his study and sit down. He shut the door behind them and crossed the room slowly and portentously; then, standing with his back to the window, and talking very earnestly, he started to try to bring home to the boys the enormity of their offense. He spoke at length and used difficult words. At one stage he said, "Of course, I know you are only boys," and Wheeler-Brown knowing the battle was won, ceased to pay even the perfunctory attention he had managed so far. Carter continued the lecture, apparently oblivious of the fact that the boys were making only a hollow pretense of listening. Long words they did not understand produced a soporific effect and they soon lost the thread altogether. Towards the end of the harangue, Carter suggested that the Almighty Himself was displeased with their behavior. This was the climax and it produced quite an effect—on Carter himself, who decided he might have been a little too fierce. He came abruptly to a halt and hastily shooed the boys from the room, placing a comforting hand on the last two shoulders to disappear. He wondered if they would be able to sleep.

Claydon Court had at one time been the fulfillment of a Victorian mill-owner's social ambition. It had been erected regardless of cost, complete with battlements, turrets and Gothic windows, by a would-be squire who spoke with a Lancashire accent. He had lived in it for ten years, snubbed by the local gentry who found he could not ride, and laughed at behind his back by his class-conscious servants. On his death his homely wife elected to return to the family house near Bolton and the Claydon estate was sold.

Outrageous even by contemporary standards, this red-brick white elephant could have but one destiny: in the course of time it became a school. And in this new role its defects became virtues: its remote position ensured privacy and endeared it to those parents not anxious to see too much of their offspring; its draughty corridors, to which the Lanca-shire laird probably owed his premature demise, were ideal for teaching boys the art of self-discipline; and its myriads of rooms housed more than eighty boys and most of the staff with ease.

When Warren heard that the boys concerned in the bulb-throwing incident had escaped scot-free, he was very angry indeed. For a while he went about in an explosive, tight-lipped state saying little. Then, three days after the journey from London when the preliminary confusion of the beginning of term was dying down, he decided he must discuss the affair with somebody and, after debating who this should be, went to pay an evening call on Peter Maitland.

Including the new Head, there were five unmarried masters on the staff. Carter had a suite of rooms in the eastern wing of the house on the first floor usually reached by the Big Door, a massive set of double doors at the head of an ornate staircase. The remainder of this floor was taken up with dormitories and the matrons' rooms. The four other resident masters had their studies and bedrooms on the second floor and were adjacent to one another.

Maitland, who taught English, was in his mid-thirties and had been at Claydon for several years. He had a passion for collecting, anything from butterflies to beer mats, and this usually gave him common ground with the boys. As he knocked, Warren was wondering what the latest craze might be.

He opened the door in response to Maitland's invitation

and walked into a study littered with books and clothes; the resident was obviously unpacking. In one corner a heavy form, its back toward him, bent over a saucepan brewing coffee on a small electric stove.

"Hullo, Peter, I'm just in time I see. I'll have mine black, please."

As Warren started to speak, Maitland spilt the milk and a sizzling sound accompanied his muttered curses. He restored the saucepan to its place and turned around, his face flushed from bending. Though still young, his waistline was not so slim as it might have been and this, together with the heavy flesh rounding his face, suggested liberal living.

"Sit down, John. Sorry about the language, I'm not so good at the household chores."

Maitland cleared a chair by the simple process of pushing a pile of books and clothes on to the floor, then offered a box of cigarettes from the mantelpiece.

"Come on, Peter, wake up. You know I don't smoke."

"Sorry, force of habit. I haven't got used to the idea of another term yet." He took a cigarette for himself and sank heavily into the armchair opposite Warren. The hair graying at his temples lent a certain distinction to balance his air of dissipation.

"Well now, what's up? You haven't got any cricket matches for me to umpire yet, I hope. I did my stint last year. Get Gregory to help you out, he's younger than I am." He flicked a match toward the fireplace.

"No, not yet, but you'll have to do some before the end of the season. Besides, you ought to have some fresh air."

Warren smiled, but inwardly he was wondering what was wrong with Maitland. He had come into the room intending to launch out on a searing attack on the Head, but he was so struck by Maitland's apparent preoccupation and nervousness that he stopped himself. He had never offered him a cigarette before; his conversation seemed forced; and Warren could have sworn that he had jumped when he spilt the milk. The unpleasant smell still hung in the air.

Maitland interrupted his train of thought: "What did you think of the bulb business?"

Warren was immediately jerked back to his grievance. He replied with a question: "Do you know what Carter's done to the little devils?"

Maitland opened his mouth, but Warren forestalled him.

"Nothing! Absolutely nothing! It's incredible that a man can be so stupid. Five boys damage public property, behaving like breakouts from Borstal, and what happens?" Warren snorted and arched his eyebrows. "He talks to them for ten minutes, and he uses such ridiculous words that the boys don't understand one in ten. Wheeler-Brown told me so. That is meant to teach self-discipline!" He paused to draw breath, but not long enough for any interruption. "I can't imagine a worse start to the term. Where's his authority? And what's more important, where's ours? Any headmaster who doesn't support his staff is letting a school down. I can't remember Carter supporting anybody since he's been here."

"Just the opposite. If the boys can't get round us, they know jolly well they can get around him." Maitland at last managed to speak, but Warren hardly noticed.

"I'm beginning to wonder if it's worth while trying to keep any discipline at all. But if we don't we're letting everybody down. What about the wretched boys, and their parents who are paying through the nose to have them brought up properly? What about our own standards?"

"Don't get so worked up, John," said Maitland, who seemed to have relaxed in response to Warren's excitement. "The world outside is changing. It soon won't matter a damn whether anyone is brought up properly or not. You're defending a lost cause. In fact, I'd go so far as to say that if we teach this lot the traditional virtues they're going to be sadly handicapped in a devil-take-the-hindmost world. Make your peace with it. I did a long time ago. Oh, blast," he ended lamely, as the milk in the saucepan surged up and overflowed. He got up and bent down to the scene of the crisis.

A knock came at the door. Again Maitland seemed to jump slightly.

"Come in," he called, and Warren could not decide what emotions were uppermost on his face when the door opened and Gregory, the recent staff replacement, came in. A curious combination of relief and anger momentarily crossed his features.

Gregory only wanted to borrow some sugar and went off as quickly as he had come. But Maitland was obviously relieved that he had not stayed longer, so taking the hint Warren excused himself and got up to leave. He was actually holding the door handle when a quick light tap heralded another visitor. The new arrival did not wait for a reply and Warren had to step back hastily to avoid being hit as the door swung open and Linda Grant, the assistant matron, came into the room.

"Oh, I'm sorry, Mr. Warren, I didn't know you were there." Taken aback, she hesitated. Standing in the doorway, a bright red dress contrasting with her dark hair, full lips slightly parted and her eyes wide, she was at her most attractive. She was pretty in a rather obvious way; a perceptive producer might have cast her as a soubrette, albeit one from whom he would first have to scrape a veneer of sophistication and a too-blatant sexuality.

"That's all right, Miss Grant. My fault, I expect. See you later, Peter." Warren, nervous and never at ease with women, particularly those as fetching as Linda Grant, retired. But even as he breathed a sigh of relief at being spared longer conversation with her, he wondered why she had entered Maitland's room with so little ceremony.

Inside the study, Maitland and Linda watched the door close.

"Thank God he's gone," exclaimed Linda. "I almost blurted something out before I saw him."

"What did Carter say?"

"Much the same as he did to you."

"Bloody puritan. If we don't move swiftly, we shall lose the lot. But money's not the only thing. Come here." He patted his knee. "You can't expect to get away unmolested with a skirt as short as that."

CHAPTER FOUR

THE daily routine at Claydon was set in motion when the matron sounded the rising bell; and this was symbolic, for Mrs. Quail was the one indispensable member of the staff. She had been at Claydon since the war and during that time her calm efficiency had acquired for her a key role in the life of the school.

Carter was Mrs. Quail's third headmaster and he was already leaning on her as heavily as had his predecessors; indeed more heavily, for the two previous Heads had been married, but Carter was not, so he depended on his matron to play the hostess whenever he entertained. The result was that Mrs. Quail had further consolidated an already impregnable position.

Alison Quail was sixty, but looked nearer forty. She was tall and thin, and her taut, wiry body was topped by an impressive head of black hair; only here and there did a gray wisp betray her age. Her features were rugged and commanding in an unfeminine, almost military way; she had never been beautiful, but she carried an air of authority none could miss. Her inevitable tweeds and hand-knitted stock-

22

ings suggested a hike in the Highlands or a perpetual point-to-point.

She was something of an enigma. It was generally known that she was a widow and it was rumored that she had lost a son during the war, but apart from these scraps of information nothing was known. She did nothing to encourage friendship and was on terms of the strictest formality with both masters and boys. The staff respected her; the boys feared her. With Carter's discipline being so weak, Mrs. Quail was one of the last deterrents remaining; a sharp reprimand from her achieved more than ten minutes' prosy exhortation from the Headmaster.

Mrs. Quail rang the rising bell on the Wednesday of the third week of term quite unaware that she was inaugurating a most evenful day. Within seconds the dormitories were astir and after making a swift tour of inspection she went down to the dining-hall to check that breakfast would be on time. Downstairs her arrival was greeted by a flurry of activity on the part of the slatternly kitchen staff.

She brought an atmosphere of vitality and energy where previously there had been only indolent lethargy. She strode about the room; apprehensively, all eyes followed her. She found some dirty cutlery, burned toast hastily pushed to the bottom of the pile, and a dead fly in a sugar bowl. "Not good enough," she barked, indicting the whole kitchen as she spun around.

Seconds later she was speeding upstairs again, leaving a humming kitchen behind her; she had a shrewd suspicion that some of the senior boys had gone back to bed. Thus did 'the Q,' as she was known to the boys, carry the burden of the school.

Breakfast was at eight o'clock and the boys stood behind their benches until Carter had said grace. Before the new Head's appointment, this had been the responsibility of the duty master, but Carter had decided that the blessing of bread at the first meal of the day was the Headmaster's prerogative and so both master and boys now had to wait for him to appear each day.

"For what we are about to receive may the Lord make us truly thankful."

The last word died away and the dining-hall burst into a cacophony of conversation and clashing cutlery. Begbie, the duty master, sat down resignedly to his most uncomfortable breakfast of the week. Carter surveyed the scene benignly for a moment or two and then set off in search of his own breakfast in his private dining room. As he closed the door, the confusion of sound faded behind him and his eye fell on a ray of blue sunlight streaming through one of the hideous panes of colored glass that decorated his front door. For a moment he was taken aback by the sheer ugliness of the glass, then the sun reminded him that he was intending to speak to Mrs. Quail about the possibility of starting school swimming.

The month of May was three weeks old and so far had been quite cloudless. Each succeeding day had pushed the temperature graph higher in the geography room and there were astonished reports from the Air Ministry roof. The boys had been clamoring for an early start to swimming almost since the first day of term and as long as their demands were not unreasonable Carter always tried to satisfy them. He found Mrs. Quail in the sewing-room.

"Good morning, Matron—er—there was one small matter I was going to mention." The Headmaster was always a long time getting to the point, as Mrs. Quail knew from experience. She said nothing but waited expectantly.

"Er, with regard to the business of the swimming pool. The boys have been asking if they can start swimming soon. As it's my first summer term I'm not quite sure what happens so I thought I would come and seek your advice. I know it's early in the term, but this weather really is unprecedented. . . ." Nervously fiddling with a pile of undarned socks, Carter rambled on, carefully weighing the pros and cons of the case. Would the parents like it? What would happen if anyone caught penumonia?

Mrs. Quail, who disliked wasting time and whose impatience at this stream of consciousness had been steadily growing, interrupted the flow: "It is an excellent idea that the boys should swim, Mr. Carter. It's quite warm enough and they might just as well go in now as wait until June when it will probably pour with rain." She moved slightly, indicating that as far as she was concerned the decision was taken and the interview at an end.

"Yes, yes, I'm sure you're right, Matron. I just wonder though. Perhaps I ought to ask some other members of the staff?"

"Just as you wish, Mr. Carter."

For Mrs. Quail the matter was over and she started sorting some laundry. She knew that the Head would probably take a consensus of opinion before finally deciding. Only on his pet hobby-horse of discipline was he obdurately opposed to advice.

With many apologies for disturbing her, Carter left the room and went to breakfast. He had already decided to shelve the problem until the mid-morning break when he would consult the remainder of the staff. Nevertheless, whether he realized it or not, the matron's firm voice had given him the decision he required. He still heard the echo of her forceful opinion as he slowly descended the stairs: "It is an excellent idea that the boys should swim." The swimming bath would be opened; the boys would swim. Mrs. Quail had unwittingly fulfilled the next stage of Fate's inexorable plan.

* * *

During the break the Head spoke to the staff and found them in complete agreement with the matron. By the end of break the news was abroad among the boys and a general air of excitement prevailed. It is possible that this contributed to the failure of Mr. Jordon's history period with IIb.

Dennis Jordon was a competent historian who, like so many of his race, knew one period well and others hardly at all. He had taken a good degree at Cambridge and had drifted into teaching partly because he thought he would be useless at anything else and partly because he hoped to do some historical research in the holidays. Recently his work had gathered speed and he now hoped to have a small book ready for publication the following year.

A successful historian, however, does not necessarily make a successful schoolmaster and Dennis Jordon did not enjoy imparting his knowledge to small boys. His patience was short and he had no time for the puerile red-herrings drawn so obviously and so frequently across his path. And he had trouble with discipline. This had been bad enough in his form room before the change in headmasters; now it was at times sheer bedlam.

On this occasion, he strode purposefully into his form room determined to take the initiative. "Before we go on to something new," he opened, "we'll just see how much you remember about what we did last time."

Jordon ran a chalky finger around his ill-fitting collar and glared balefully around the room. He was still in his thirties but gave the impression of premature decay; his clothes were old and shapeless, so dull as to be almost without color, and his scarecrow-like figure invited the cruel caricature of small boys; his face already had that haggard, leathery quality associated with age.

He adjusted his spectacles—these, too, gave the impression of being slightly lop-sided—and prepared for battle. "Anderson, what can you remember about Empson and Dudley?"

Anderson remembered almost nothing. They sounded rather like a comedy team he had seen on television, but felt that the time had not yet come for jokes. Someone else volunteered some tolerably accurate information to rescue him. But the bombardment was on again. One lesson Jordon had learned was that pauses should be avoided at all costs.

"What was the name of Henry VII's eldest son?"

Two or three hands went up.

"Ward major?"

"Arthur, sir. He died young and that's why Henry VIII became king, sir."

"You have the germs of truth, Ward." Jordon was disappointed that his trick question had misfired. It gave the enemy a chance to counter-attack.

A rather dirty hand rose. "Excuse me, sir, is this Arthur the one who had the round table?"

Jordon blinked; he disliked this sort of question. He was never sure if his leg was being pulled or whether information was genuinely being sought. He found no clue in the voice of his questioner, which was perplexed, or his face, which was straight. A titter wormed its way around the form.

Jordon bent forward over his desk and studied the boy with a pained expression. To the class this represented the successful completion of stage one of the operation. He said: "Are you as dim as you lead me to believe?"

Now it was the turn of the boy to look pained, while the rest of the form shouted: "Yes, sir, he is, sir!"

"Be quiet. There is no need for anybody else to speak. One idiot in the form is quite sufficient. Right—er—now we'll get on. Why did Henry VIII divorce Catherine of Aragon?"

A forest of hands shot up.

"Clarke?"

"Because he wanted to chop off her head, sir."

"Imbecile." Jordon's voice, hitherto quiet and he hoped sarcastic, began to rise. Desperately he turned to another hand. "Yes, Brown?"

"Did they use an axe or a sword, sir?"

"Yes, sir, did they have to hold her down?"

Another answered: "No, that was Ann Boleyn. They had to chase her around the block with the executioner chopping at her with the axe. Isn't that right, sir?"

"Silence!" shouted Jordon, at last managing to interrupt the flood of historical inaccuracy. "I will not have everybody talking at once. And I will only answer sensible questions."

"Mine *was* sensible, sir," said a hurt voice. "Did they behead Catherine of Aragon with an axe or a sword, sir?" The gory details of death and torture so dear to the heart of every schoolboy once more came to the fore.

Jordon recognized the symptoms of disorder. He was fast losing control of both the form and himself. He struggled to steady his temper. "You are quite wrong in believing that Catherine of Aragon was executed, Brown. She was divorced and died naturally. Only Ann Boleyn and Catherine Howard were beheaded."

"Why, sir?" As always, Jordon's love of historical truth was leading him into deep waters.

"Well—Henry didn't think they were good wives."

"What did they do wrong, sir?"

Jordon hesitated and shuffled his notes. This was tricky ground with twelve-year-old boys. He had already had difficulty that morning explaining why Elizabeth is called the Virgin Queen and had no intention of getting involved with the indiscretions of Norris and Culpepper.

The boys seized on that pause. "I don't think you know, sir."

"Shall I look it up for you, sir?"

The period was rapidly disintegrating. Jordan stood up; he scratched his head vigorously, making his hair stick out at all angles; his spectacles drooped forlornly. To the boys he was ludicrous; to any disinterested onlooker he would have been pathetic.

Only one boy had not contributed to the general confusion. He sat alone in one corner, utterly absorbed in something hidden behind a large pile of books.

Jordon suddenly became aware of this solitary oasis of silence. He strode across the room until he stood over the boy. The remainder turned to watch.

"And *what* do you think you are doing?"

The offender jerked upright, conscious of the presence looming above him. No answer was required; Mr. Jordon could see quite well what he was doing. In his hand was a sheath-knife, sharp and bright; on the desk, standing out clearly among the ink stains of several generations, was a very recently carved letter 'M.' Small chippings of wood completed the indictment.

"I'll have that, thank you, Manton."

Manton relinquished the knife.

"Leave the room at once and report to the Big Door."

Manton left and the boys were silent. The phrase, 'the Big Door,' even when uttered by Mr. Jordon and even though little happened there any more, was still sufficient to bring peace to a form. By crushing the one boy who had taken no part in the disturbance, Jordan had temporarily averted a complete breakdown of discipline. And somehow he had kept his temper.

He returned to his desk; he could face the boys again. He said: "Now I think we will return to the sixteenth century."

On his desk, razor sharp, the confiscated sheath-knife glinted in the warm sun streaming through the window.

CHAPTER FIVE

THE term was closing in on Carter. All around him he felt the hostility building up, the familiar symptoms of distrust, just as he had in the two previous terms. Warren was at the center of the opposition, he knew that, but after all he was Second Master, so if he thought things were going wrong he had a right, almost a duty, to say so. Carter was eminently fair. But Warren was not alone. Jordon undoubtedly blamed him for the disorder endemic in his form room, and Begbie, casual dilettante though he was, seemed to find the discipline problem less amusing than he had done. Mrs. Quail, true to character, said little, but Carter detected bleak animosity beneath her taut, impassive exterior. Even the newcomer Gregory, his own appointment, who was supposedly favorable to forward-looking ideas, seemed disillusioned now he saw them in practice. As for Maitland and Miss Grant . . . they, of course, raised another problem, one that he felt even less capable of handling.

And there were other headaches. A village shopkeeper was complaining, apparently justifiably, that two of the boys had been shoplifting. Then only yesterday a little boy in his first term had run away and reached Taunton before being caught by the police. Slightly less important, but worrying nevertheless, was a letter from a father who wanted his son caned. He had sent his son to Claydon, he asserted, to receive a gentleman's education, and that included being beaten if he misbehaved. He certainly was not going to continue to pay the fees, heavy ones at that, for him to be brought up a milksop. Carter had received several letters in this vein, but this was trickier than most for the parent in question owned a nearby estate and had served in the same regiment as at least one of the Governors.

The one cheerful spot in an otherwise depressing outlook was the letter he had received that morning from a firm of publishers accepting for publication the typescript of a book he had been working on for some time. It was good for his self-esteem; recently his failure to carry the staff with him, not to mention the lack of response on the part of the boys, had led him to question his ability to run the school on what he regarded as the right lines, something he had never done before. Furthermore, he hoped that once the news of his literary success got abroad it might gain a little respect from those who had been notably lacking in it so far.

As he sat at the desk in his study mulling his problems over, Carter became aware of shouting and laughter drifting across the park and in at his open window. For a moment he was puzzled. Then he remembered that swimming had now started and realized that the pool was the source of the hubbub. He remembered also that he had promised to pay a visit on the opening day. Although he had little natural interest in the sporting side of school life, he felt gestures of this sort were worth making; so, pushing aside the draft of his reply to the father of the uncaned boy, he got up from his desk and set off toward the sound of distant revelry.

Down at the pool the masters, standing statuesque at

different points around the edge, were trying hard to look enthusiastic as the boys leaped in and out of the clear green water. Glistening bodies, lithe and agile, soaked up the warm sunshine; above them, funneling upward from the natural amphitheater in which the pool had been built, rose the colossal noise inseparable from the activities of small boys. No one paid much attention when the Head opened the door in the surrounding fence and stepped on to the well-kept grass inside the enclosure. He was an unimpressive figure and, unlike some headmasters, caused no stir as he moved about the school. He put his hands in his pockets, hunched his shoulders slightly, and looked around for someone to talk to.

Dennis Jordon, arms folded and head bent, was standing by himself looking thoroughly bored. He had no interest in swimming but felt it his duty to make a token appearance on such a festive occasion. He was just wondering how much longer he needed to stay when he became conscious of Carter at his elbow. He was not particularly pleased that Carter had singled him out for attention, but he put a brave face on it. He did not dislike the new Head as much as his colleagues and sometimes thought they were too hard on him. He saw him as a misguided philanthropist rather than a wanton meddler, a tolerant view that came near to the truth.

"I'm sorry about the bother with Manton, Dennis. I've stopped him swimming today and he will not be allowed out next weekend. I always think it's best to take away their privileges, don't you?"

Jordon made a noise which might have been interpreted as assent and ran a nervous hand through his hair. A long pause followed.

"I had a piece of good news this morning."

"Really, Headmaster?"

"Yes, I've just had a book accepted. It's the first time I've managed to get into print."

Jordon showed mild interest. Inwardly he wondered what on earth Carter had written about and was tempted to ask if it was educational theory.

"History, you know. I read History up at Oxford. One of these days I shall be coming to take a few periods for you," said Carter jocularly.

"I had no idea you were an historian, Headmaster. What's your particular interest?"

"The Civil War. I've always found it fascinating."

"And you've done some original work?"

"Well, not really," replied Carter deprecatingly. "I've used secondary sources mostly, but a lot of the documents have been published so it's easy to get at them. You see the Civil War is only the background. My real subject is the appearance of revolutionary ideas among the ordinary people. As you know, the Civil War was a struggle between the propertied classes, but once the Royalists had been defeated all sorts of egalitarian ideas were let loose among the rank and file of the parliamentary army, ideas that haven't . . ."

"What exactly is the title of your book?" cut in Jordan with uncharacteristic rudeness.

"*The Levellers.* That was the name given them by their enemies, of course. They didn't really want complete equality but they said some strange things for their day and age, and they certainly frightened the landowners. Do you know that Cromwell was fêted like a hero after he had crushed them at Burford?"

Carter was enthusiastic now. He went on: "Professor Rescinowicz of Harvard—and you know the Americans know more about our Civil War than we do ourselves—Professor Rescinowicz has been kind enough to read my typescript and make some helpful comments. In fact, I think his approval probably helped persuade the publishers to accept it." He rambled on, explaining the construction of the book, quoting from a lively Lilburne pamphlet, and showing why he could not subscribe to Professor T's well-known interpretation of the Leveller movement. "These men were individuals," he said, his voice rising slightly. "They don't fit into . . ."

Then he looked at Jordon, and his voice faltered and died away. Quite suddenly Jordon looked ill. His face was white, his eyes, staring fixedly through his drooping spectacles, were glazed. In a brief moment of time he seemed to have become an old man.

"What's the matter, Dennis? Are you ill?"

"No . . . no . . . it's nothing, Mr. Carter. I'll be all right in a minute." And without another word he walked slowly away around the side of the bath, his head lowered and his gait more of a shuffle than usual.

"Odd," mused Carter, as he watched him. "I hope there's nothing seriously wrong with him." Although he was anything but a callous man, he was already wondering whether he might have yet another master to replace. Too many staff changes looked bad in one's first year; the Governors were apt to ask awkward questions.

He looked round to see if anyone had noticed his strange meeting with Jordon, but no one was paying any attention at all. The boys were far too preoccupied. Warren was taking part in an impromptu race; Gregory, kneeling perilously near the edge, was encouraging a non-swimmer to take his first trembling strokes; Maitland and Begbie, their backs toward him, stood deep in conversation.

"Coming in, sir?" A boy's dripping face appeared over the edge of the pool.

"No, not today, boys. I may think about it later on."

"Come on, sir! Mr. Warren's in sir. Come and have a race with him, sir."

"Perhaps tomorrow. I'll see." Slightly worried lest the boys should continue to pester him, and even more worried that he might not be able to resist much longer, Carter turned away and returned thoughtfully to the school.

Later that afternoon Begbie and Maitland found themselves alone together in the staff room waiting for tea. Begbie was obviously furious about something, but he managed to restrain himself while the maid brought in tea and the inevitable slab cake.

As the door closed, he exploded: "Do you know what happened when I blew the whistle for the boys to come out?"

Maitland, who seemed preoccupied, grunted sympathetically and poured two cups of tea.

"A few of the weaker brethren came out, but a lot of them just swam out to the middle of the pool and Braybrooke took it as a signal to dive in again."

"That child is competing for the title of The Most Odious Boy in the School. I nearly clobbered him myself yesterday. It's all quite typical, of course."

"I suddenly noticed just how bad the discipline is. And I realized that John hasn't been exaggerating. I felt quite helpless."

"I suppose they came out eventually."

"Just about. They crawled out at a snail's pace smirking to themselves. It was all extremely unpleasant. Damn it, Peter, they're only boys and of course they'll break rules if they can. From a boy's point of view that's all rules are for. But if a school's going to have rules—and I for one am not staying in one that hasn't—then the staff has got to enforce them. Otherwise both the staff and the rules are a laughing stock."

"Why don't you go and tell Carter what you think of him while you're in the mood? You're too gentlemanly by half—and the day of the gentleman is over, Mark. I'm always telling you that."

"No, I'll cool down a bit first, I don't want to be rash. But I shall have a word with him in the morning. Not that it will do the slightest good," he added gloomily.

The door opened and Jordon came in; he was still ashen.

"Hullo, Dennis. What are you doing here? I suppose your wife has kicked you out at last and you want some tea."

Jordon ignored Maitland's heavy facetiousness. "Here's another contribution to the armory," he said, holding up the knife he had confiscated earlier in the day. "I found Manton hacking his name for posterity on his desk."

He dropped the knife into the box kept for confiscations, turned abruptly and left the room.

"What's up with old Dennis today? That was a bit brusque, wasn't it?" said Begbie.

"The boys are getting him down, I expect. The din reaches me through the wall and I sometimes think I ought to go and give him a hand."

"I thought we had got rid of all those sheath-knives. That is one thing Carter has tried to do."

"Not with any resounding success," rejoined Maitland.

Carter himself came into the room shortly afterward and the conversation flagged. The Head's appearance always had the same effect, but he continued to have his tea in the staff room. He felt he was keeping in touch, though only the vaguest platitudes passed across the table in his presence. To Begbie's dismay, Maitland excused himself almost as soon as Carter sat down and he was left to cope on his own.

"Going swimming soon, Mark?"

"Not yet, sir. I'll give the water a chance to warm up a bit first, though I must say it looked very pleasant in there today."

Begbie insisted on calling Carter 'sir' because he considered it the correct mode of address. It was his form of protest against progress; and he knew it made Carter uncomfortable.

Carter told Begbie about his book, and it was a full twenty minutes before Begbie was able to escape without appearing rude. Eventually, after what seemed an interminable lecture on the Levellers, he made his excuses and withdrew.

Carter waited a moment of two, slightly disappointed that Begbie had now shown more enthusiasm over his success, then returned to his private part of the school. As he passed his front door, he noticed that the afternoon post had been delivered. A solitary envelope lay on its face just inside the door. He picked it up and turned it over.

The moment he saw the typewritten address he knew what it was, yet his fingers automatically ripped it open and drew out the contents.

"Another one," he said aloud. "Why can't I be left in peace?"

He sat down carefully in the nearest chair. His hands were shaking.

CHAPTER SIX

THE evening drew on and the air began to cool. The days might be hot, but the chill of the nights showed that spring had not yet become high summer. As the shadows lengthened across the cricket field in front of the main school building, rooks conversed noisily in the elms above the pavilion before settling down for the night.

Hugh Gregory, pallid and not yet entirely free from the acne of adolescence, made his way down the long drive which curled away through the park. Earnest, bespectacled, and slightly stooping, he fingered the binoculars hanging around his neck; as a compulsive birdwatcher, he never stirred outside unless he was equipped for action. He was going to the village and his short legs and unathletic gait guaranteed him a walk of at least twenty minutes. But Gregory noticed neither time nor distance; for Gregory was worrying about his career.

This was no new experience for him, but it remained a protracted and painful business. He had worried about it when he had first won his place at the grammar school; then, again, it had dominated the whole of his last year at university; and now, a short time after taking his first post, he was beginning to have doubts. On a theoretical plane, as a socialist, he was wondering how to reconcile his political beliefs with a job in a private school, one of the bastions of a privileged society; on a more practical level, he was not finding teaching the simple, uncomplicated task he had hoped for. He trusted that an evening at the De Mallet Arms, oldest and most comfortable of the village pubs, would do something to clarify his ideas.

On reaching the door, he hesitated. His conscience urged him to join his proletarian comrades in the public bar; something stronger, a longing for peace and quiet, prompted him to turn to the lounge, which he found deserted. The landlord pulled him half a pint of bitter and then, to Gregory's relief, returned to the crowded buzz of the other bar. He did not feel like talking to anybody and for a moment or two did not even want to think. An empty mood had possession, not black, but gray and vague. So he was content to sit; and with any luck he would not be disturbed.

Claydon had given his ideals a sharp jolt. The prospect of bringing the light of learning to intelligent seekers of knowledge had filled him with eager anticipation. Selfishly he had hoped to enjoy it. It had come as a shock to find that small boys do not spend all their waking hours in pursuit of wisdom, and that a teaching diploma is little more than a scrap of paper when the basic problems of the form room rear their heads. He was soon at loggerheads with most of his forms and was surprised to discover he had a sharp temper, a shortcoming he had never previously suspected.

This disturbed him most of all. But he was also upset by the low morale of both staff and boys. Although he had long ago dismissed the idea of 'team spirit' as merely a cunning rallying call for the upper classes, a form of imperialistic trade unionism, he could not possibly condone the aimless air of lethargy which had replaced it under Carter's benevolent leadership. The boys seemed to have ceased to care what the masters thought of them, and the masters were fast losing all personal interest in the boys.

Carefully and precisely Gregory drank from his tankard. He held it by the handle, consciously repudiating the habits of the hearties, who seized it around the waist as though the handle did not exist.

It was not all Carter's fault, he reflected. The staff was far from ideal. Take Mrs. Quail. Strange how one always thought of her first. She was cool and efficient, of course, and frightfully 'county.' He shuddered at the thought that he was associated with somebody who was county. She could not be as hard-bitten as she made out. After all, at some time or other, a Mr. Quail had married her and, although he did not know much about women, Gregory understood that husbands looked for femininity in their wives. He seemed quite emancipated from such problems himself.

Mrs. Quail was supervising the boys' preparation for bed. Tonight, the excitement of the first day's swimming was slow to die down and there was a good deal of noise as the senior boys splashed in the washrooms. The juniors, scrubbed and inspected, were already in bed, but even in the dormitories there was still a buzz of conversation.

The matron moved swiftly around the basins, looking behind ears, stirring up the laggards and silencing any noise she considered excessive. One word was usually sufficient.

She was tired this evening for it was Linda Grant's half-day and she was coping on her own. She was looking forward to the moment when the last boy was in bed, the 'lights out' bell was rung, and she could go to her room to relax. The tail-enders received the sharp edge of her tongue

and scampered away at speed. It was noticeable that most of
her charges were going to bed slightly cleaner than usual.

And Mark Begbie. Gregory wondered vaguely what had
led him to Begbie after Mrs. Quail. It might have been the
touch of class he carried about; or perhaps it was his
characteristic languor, which made such a contrast to the
matron's constant activity. He was pleasant enough and
never seemed to cross anybody's path; but he spent too
much time considering the fashionable width of his trousers—Gregory glanced down at his own shapeless flan-
nels—and he was a snob, too. He patronized anyone who
had not been to Oxford or Cambridge. Or was that his own
red-brick sensitivity? Gregory had never before considered
the possibility that he might be a snob. It gave him a new
view of himself and he shot off at a tangent.

In his room on the second floor, low-ceilinged and still
retaining some of the warmth of the day, Mark Begbie
settled down for a comfortable evening. He had finished his
marking before supper and could now relax with a pipe and
coffee. He was still feeling aggrieved by the flouting of his
authority in the swimming bath, but trusted he would be
restored to his normal good humor by the concert being
broadcast from the Royal Festival Hall.

He opened the windows wide. With the boys on their way
to bed, there was no shouting to drift up from below, a
constant throb of noise which drove him to keep them shut
all day. For a few moments he looked out across the park,
smiling slightly at the outline of Victorian crenellation
clearly defined in front of the school.

Then he turned on the wireless. A crescendo of applause
announced Krovsky's appearance and Begbie sat down to
await the gloomy opening of Beethoven's *Leonora No. 3.*.

* * *

When Gregory considered a problem, he liked to arrange all the pros and cons in mental pigeon-holes. It was his boast that he could come to a decision quite unaffected by emotion or any other incalculable human factor. Yet tonight his filing system was not functioning properly. Every time he tried to arrange his data, something dragged him back to the unpleasant atmosphere at the school. He sensed that the situation was dangerously unbalanced, that the tension, distrust, even—dare he think it?—hatred, were moving to a crisis. He could not account for the feeling, but it made concentration on his own personal matters very difficult.

Who was weaving this entanglement of suspicion? It was difficult to pin any one person down; each had played his part in his own way. Even he had added to it, keeping himself at a nervous distance from his colleagues. An individual or two stood out. What did he know, for instance, about Maitland?

At first glance he was a beer-swilling hearty, a schoolboy who had never grown up. But there was more to him than that. A streak of cynicism made a mockery of his adoption of a teaching career; and he was capable of deep personal animosity. He certainly disliked Carter, there could be no doubt about that. Apart from Warren, no one had been so outspoken in his antagonism toward the head. Except, perhaps, Linda Grant. Now she *was* feminine, even Gregory could see that.

Begbie lay back in his chair, one leg cocked over the arm. A curl of smoke wisped slowly up from his pipe before bending toward the open window. The sheer beauty of the clarinet playing Florestan's prison air found him completely content.

He put out a hand to turn up the volume as the overture

gathered momentum. This was full-blooded music; he wanted every drop of emotion. He closed his eyes as the thunderous coda reverberated around in the room and soared out of the window. He hoped Maitland next door did not mind the noise.

But although Beethoven's paean of hope and freedom penetrated the wall, Maitland did not mind at all. For Maitland was not there.

CHAPTER SEVEN

SOMETHING captured Gregory's attention. He sat still, suddenly aware of voices in the other bar. Yes, there it was again. From the midst of the confused hubbub came a voice he knew. It was Dennis Jordon.

Gregory got up and went to the corner of the bar, whence he could see the greater part of the other room. He had never seen Jordon anywhere near the village pub before, but he was now deep in an argument with a man who looked like a farm laborer. And, there could be no doubt about it, Jordon was very nearly tight. Gregory smiled and sat down. He did not usually find drunkenness amusing, but Jordon was different. It would probably do him good, poor chap.

Jordon, he reflected, had not contributed greatly to the unpleasant school atmosphere. Living in an erudite world of his own, he was a victim of the situation rather than a creator of it. Gregory was sorry for him and he had reason: he saw in Dennis Jordon the image of himself in ten or fifteen years' time. It was a sobering thought; and it brought him sharply back to his own career.

If he thought he could do no better than Jordon, he would

hand in his resignation tomorrow. If he was to stay in teaching, then he was going to be a success—like Warren. Warren might be old-fashioned, but he was a tower of strength in the school. He consistently produced outstanding results in Classic, while his ability to nurture skill and enthusiasm in rugger and cricket teams led to one fine season after another. Yet Gregory gave his admiration to Warren only grudgingly. For Warren, pillar of privilege, supporter of straight bats, stiff upper lips and no-sneaking codes, symbolized all that Gregory despised. He was decadent, and Gregory's Leftist intellectualism rebelled.

Moreover, Warren had much to do with the impossible situation in the school. It was he who mirrored and multiplied the grievances of the staff; it was he who could find no shred of patience to await the outcome of the Head's schemes.

Gregory's glass was empty. He ordered a refill—his third. This, he decided, really would have to be the last.

Warren was marking and he was going to be at it for some time. A neat pile of closed exercise books on his right represented work completed; a much larger stack on his left, open, had yet to be started. He was dealing with a dull form and his red Biro hovered threateningly over the page. His brow creased, he muttered to himself.

"Vulpes in agros cucurrerat. . . . Idiot, Crane . . . cucurrerant." The Biro dug into the paper.

Through the open window, the ill-defined strains of the London Sympathy Orchestra drifted across from Begbie's room. Warren glanced up, momentarily distracted. The trumpet call heralding the arrival of Don Fernando caught his ear. Although he knew little about music, he often had it on in the background while he concentrated on something else, so he listened as the overture reached its triumphant conclusion, then, when the final chords died away and merged with appreciative applause, he got up and turned on his own wireless. He might as well do all he could to make IIIb's ghastly Latin palatable.

Out of the corner of his ear, as it were, Warren heard the announcement that the next work would be Brahms' Second Piano Concerto. The formidable red Biro was already lacerating an untidy and inaccurate page produced by Payne minimus.

Once on the subject of Warren, Gregory moved naturally on to Carter. It was odd that he had not considered him before: that in itself reflected his unimpressive personality.

In a mild way Gregory disliked the Head, but not for the reasons that had come to be conventional. In fact, he sympathized with his progressive ideas and understood what he was aiming at, which was more than could be said of anyone else. No, his antipathy was for Carter himself. He was weak and ineffectual, meek and self-effacing, and there was something intensely irritating about his obvious longing to be liked. It was not so much that he disliked him, Gregory decided, it was just that he had no respect for the man.

Carter pushed away his plate and untucked the napkin from the top of his waistcoat. His solitary supper over, he had arrived at the time of day he usually reserved for relaxation with a book. The boys were in bed and nothing much could go wrong with the capable Mrs. Quail on duty. Now if it were Linda Grant it would be different. . . .

He was about to sit down in an armchair by the window when something occurred to him. The swimming bath had been opened, but had anyone remembered to check the chlorine content? Of course, it was not his job, but it would be his responsibility if anything went wrong; already he saw headlines in a national paper. Had the groundsman remembered? He probably had, but old Gregg was past seventy and could not always be relied on.

Torn between *Pride and Prejudice* and conscience, Carter unhesitatingly obeyed the latter. Some of the juniors would be swimming in the mid-morning break if the weather held, and the water must be fit for them. Procrastination was at an end; he put down his book and set off for the pool, wishing that chlorine was not such powerful stuff but congratulating himself on keeping it locked out of the boys' way.

Gregory's final beer lasted some time but did not help to clarify his ideas. Just the opposite, in fact; he was not used to drinking and he was feeling the effects of his pint and a half. He stood up, put the glass down on the bar with exaggerated care, and went outside. As he stepped out into the cool of the evening, he realized that he had not really considered his own personal future at all. Somehow it did not seem to matter. The disagreeable situation at the school was dominant. And it was more than disagreeable, it was frightening. . . .

Initially, he had thought the village street was empty, but as he stood in the doorway of the pub he slowly became aware of a strange sound and a figure sitting fifty yards away on a bench at the edge of the Green. It was hunched up, apparently immobile, its head bent forward. Without thinking, Gregory walked toward it and was barely twenty-five yards away before he realized who it was. It was Dennis Jordon and as he drew nearer he saw that he was not immobile. For Jordon was crying uncontrollably with sobs that racked his whole frame.

Silently, feeling an interloper at a private grief, Gregory retreated. He did not turn his head until he came to a bend in the road. Then he looked back and, even as he watched, Jordon stood up, wiped his spectacles, and set off up the village street.

Had it not been that he was shortly to see something else, something he always found quite irresistible, Gregory might have puzzled longer over Jordon's curious outburst.

CHAPTER EIGHT

THE Royal Festival Hall was crowded and Anna Kauper, the young Hungarian playing the Brahms concerto, was not feeling well. The heat was oppressive; her dress was too tight; and she was wondering what had made her choose Brahms for her first London appearance.

Above her, calm and compelling, towered Krovsky's bulky figure. His baton measured the six beats of the bar; the long sensitive fingers of his left hand caressed the first violins as they expanded the main theme of the *Andante*: he radiated confidence.

There was a humming in her ears now. But she must go on; she could not possibly stop in the middle of the movement. The keys, black and white, merged in front of her eyes and she was aware that she could not read the marker's name on the upturned piano lid. Yet somehow, through the haze, she could see Krovsky's remorseless baton. She followed it; she felt her head beating time. She could still hear the orchestra but it did not sound in the same hall. Her hands, remote and detached, were still playing.

They were performing mechanically, without delicacy, without sensitivity, but they were not letting her down.

She swayed forward and felt rather than saw the conductor look at her sharply. She must make an effort; the movement was nearly over, just twenty more bars and she would be at the end. Why hadn't she chosen Mozart? K.488 would have done admirably. "A lady's concerto," her teacher had said.

Her hands and arms, drilled by years of practice, followed the beat. They were working at the last bars now; the ordeal was nearly over.

Begbie stirred in his armchair. This Kauper girl wasn't doing the B flat major justice. Listen to that shoddy phrasing! A pity, she had been quite promising in the first two movements; but this *Andante* was too pedestrian for words. It made him feel uncomfortable.

"Just another foreigner bitten off more than she can chew," he reflected. "When will they learn that Brahms needs stamina?" He got up to boil some more milk; he drank coffee endlessly in the evenings.

The music stumbled to a halt. There was a sudden jangle, as though a large number of piano keys had been depressed indiscriminately. The audience buzzed with suppressed conversation.

Begbie paused, saucepan and milk jug in either hand. There followed a moment or two of apparent confusion before an embarrassed B.B.C. announcer reported that Miss Anna Kauper had become indisposed and that he was returning listeners to the studio.

"As I thought," mused Begbie, "Brahms needs stamina."

* * *

Gregory reached the main gates and his pace slowed. As he turned into the drive, he noticed that the Lodge, where the Jordons lived, had a light on. Against the blind he could see the blurred outline of Jordon's wife and he wondered what part she had played in the scene he had recently witnessed. Like most of his colleagues, he had little time for Alice Jordan, a small hard woman with few redeeming qualities.

He continued up the drive, then, on the spur of the moment, feeling he would like to delay his return to the school a little longer, he turned off on to the grass intending to follow a circuitous route across the park. The light was beginning to fade, but the main features of the park were still distinct. To his left stood the school, partly veiled by the trees round the cricket field; on the field itself old Gregg, who seemed to have taken too literally a Victorian father's injunction to labor from dawn to dusk, was pushing a hand-mower. Ahead, the top of its surrounding fence just visible above a rise in the ground, lay the swimming pool. Always to the right, dark in the gathering twilight, the Long Gallow Woods. . . .

A brief flash of red low down near the edge of the woods, so swift as to be barely discernible, caught Gregory's attention. Automatically his hands went to his binoculars; blinking, he scanned the grass fringing the trees. To begin with he could see nothing, then the line of his mouth creased into a tight, nervous smile. "Yes," he breathed. "Yes . . . I thought so."

And, clutching his binoculars, he turned sharply to his right and ran, crouching, for the nearest cover.

Henry Carter walked down to the swimming pool. It was a lovely evening and he was in no hurry. To the east the sky was already dark blue and the first ice-cold stars were appearing; to the west a warm glow lingered on the horizon, throwing into sharp relief the trees on the skyline. Away beyond the village, where lights had been showing for some time, the low line of the bald Mendip Hills stretched to the Bristol Channel.

"Bleak hills," reflected Carter; "almost ominous at night." And he thought of the sheep they had once supported and the flourishing wool trade that had long since vanished. No wonder some of the unemployed locals had been Levellers and later joined Monmouth's ill-starred rebellion, the last occasion for the waving of the Levellers' sea-green colors. Jeffreys had hanged more than a dozen on Pendon Beacon, he remembered.

He opened the door in the swimming bath enclosure and went inside. The pool, lying in a hollow, was in shadow and he walked downward into twilight as he descended the steps leading to the small wooden pavilion which served as a storage place for much of the groundsman's equipment.

For a time he searched vaguely for the cardboard box containing the test tubes and litmus paper for analyzing the water, but he could not find it. This was something of a relief, for he was not certain he knew how to use the various bits and pieces anyway. He would play for safety and assume the pool needed more chlorine.

He levered the cork out of the container, a large glass bottle surrounded by straw wedged in an iron cage, and poured some of the yellow-green liquid into a white jug kept for that purpose. Then, walking slowly and holding the jug well clear of his clothes, he began to circle the bath, every now and then splashing chlorine into the water. "Not exactly according to the manual," thought Carter primly, "but practical."

He did not hear the soft footstep behind him, and he was barely aware of any pain. But he felt the jug slip from his fingers on to the pavement and through strangely blurred vision he saw the dark water coming up to meet him.

CHAPTER NINE

THE weather held; the sun rose again on Claydon Prior. Its rays pierced the morning mist lingering in the valley and struck the great Norman tower of the ruined priory where Cluniac monks once followed the reformed routine of the Opus Dei; they glanced off the inn sign at the end of the High Street which still bore the name and arms of the eleventh-century baron who, hoping to atone for his share of the bloodshed at Hastings, had presented a handsome gift of land to the Abbot of Cluny; and then, as the sun edged its way over Pendon Beacon, they probed the wooded park of the school, where the boys, breakfast over, awaited the summons to morning assembly.

Hugh Gregory, frowning in the bright sunlight, walked out on to the terrace at the front of the school. Adjusting the *New Statesman* carefully under his left arm, he began to pull the bell rope with his right. The bell, perched high in a fanciful turret of its own, clanged noisily around the grounds.

There had been a time under the previous headmaster when the first distinctive notes were followed by an

immediate reaction from the boys; now they evoked only a
mild interest. A few younger boys who knew no better
scampered dutifully to prayers, but the majority, all sense of
urgency deadened, regarded the bell with comparative
indifference. The result was that whereas morning prayers
had formerly begun promptly at nine o'clock, it was now
rare for them to start before five past; indeed, the masters,
when they decided to attend at all, now arrived at the later
time on the grounds that if Carter had the patience to wait
for the boys, he might as well extend it to his staff. Begbie
was usually the last to arrive and today was no exception.
He was just about to turn into the assembly hall when a
small boy materialized in front of him. He had obviously
been running.

"Don't run so fast, Donovan, you won't have any breath
left for your hymn."

"Sir—I—sir—" The boy struggled for breath.

"Tell me about it afterward. You're late already." He
nearly said 'we.'

"But, sir, it's important—I've been in the swimming
bath."

Begbie was about to swivel him smartly about and propel
him into the hall when something in the boy's expression
changed his mind. His eyes were wide with surprise; a
quivering at the lips suggested he was about to cry. So
instead of pushing him into prayers, he took him out on to
the terrace and sat down with him on one of those benches
given to every school by loyal Old Boys who like to see
their names carved in prominent places.

Once out of the dark corridor and in the sunlight, Begbie
could see the boy's face properly. He was white, the sort of
white Begbie had read about but never seen.

"Now, Donovan, what's the matter?"

"Sir—I—I've been—that is, I—" Donovan, a small,

dark-haired boy, again found it had to speak, but it was words rather than breath that he was seeking now.

"Gently, now. What's up? Take it steadily, there's no hurry."

"Sir—I—there's something in the swimming pool."

"Something?"

"Someone, sir."

Begbie was nonplussed. For a moment he could not see the implication. "Do you mean that this person is swimming?"

"No, sir. It's Mr. Carter—"—a subconscious alarm sounded dully at the back of Begbie's brain and he nearly missed the crucial words—"He's in the water, sir. He—he looks as though he may be dead."

The last words rushed out and the tears which had never been far away streamed down his pale, shocked face.

The assembly hall was silent. A row of masters on uncomfortable tubular chairs faced lines of boys on uncomfortable wooden benches.

It was unlike Carter to be late; normally he was one of the first to arrive and he took pleasure in watching the school gather for its morning service. Standing benignly at his pulpit-like desk, he would wave small unwanted boys to vacant seats, all the while smiling tolerantly at latecomers. It was the one time of the day when he felt indispensable.

Maitland whispered to Warren: "Late on parade this morning. Gregory told me he missed breakfast, too."

Warren looked at his watch and grunted. He was just going to stand up and take prayers himself when he saw Begbie framed in the doorway at the back of the hall; he was beckoning urgently. Warren left his seat, his eyebrows rising in query; bat-like, his gown spread out as he swept past the boys. A shuffling of feet and posteriors accompanied a more silent swiveling of eyes.

"Something's happened, John. Come outside." There was a quality in Begbie's voice that Warren had not heard before. He followed him on to the terrace. "I've just seen Donovan. He was going to skip prayers in the swimming bath but he's had a shock. He says Carter's in the pool—he thinks he's dead."

Warren's expression did not change. He asked: "Where's Donovan?"

"I sent him off to Mrs. Quail. He was crying his eyes out."

"Do you believe him?"

"I'm afraid so. He looked dreadful."

"Well, there's only one way to find out. Let's get down there to see for ourselves."

Warren quickly took charge. He was at his best when any sort of crisis threatened and already seemed to have assimilated the impact of the news. He quickly arranged for the boys to be sent to the form rooms, then, with Begbie beside him, set off at a smart trot across the park. They ran without talking. Partly because they needed their breath to run, but largely because an odd tension had risen between them. It was born of a sense of guilt; for both men had said harsh things about Carter, both would have been delighted to have seen him removed from his post. But death was different. . . .

And there were other thoughts. Supposing he were dead—and Donovan's behavior suggested the conditional to be superfluous—how had he died? A shadow much larger than a badly run school began to loom over them. So it was not surprising that they ran in silence, their feet swishing through the damp morning grass.

They reached the door in the fence. Warren opened it. "No wonder Donovan got a shock," he said.

"My God!" exclaimed Begbie.

They ran down the grassy slope to the edge of the pool.

"Come on. We've got to get him out." Warren was still in command.

They knelt at the water's edge and heaved the body that had been Henry Carter on to the paving-stones. A pool of water slowly spread outward around him.

"He's dead," said Warren calmly. "Look at this." He pointed to a red patch glistening darkly on the sodden cloth of Carter's jacket.

Begbie had already seen it and was several yards away trying hard not to be sick. "He wasn't drowned, John," he said. He shook his head and repeated, "He wasn't drowned." Then he added: "I've never seen a dead man before."

"I'm afraid I have." A look of revulsion passed over Warren's face as he recalled the first dead German he had seen, a young Wehrmacht private in a ditch near Caen, and then his own batman blown to pieces on a badly sited gun position.

Warren stood up. "Come on, we can't do anything for him now. I'll get the school running as normally as possible. You go and phone the doctor and the police—on second thoughts you'd better get the police first, the doctor won't be much use."

Begbie carried out Warren's instructions, albeit shakily, but although he remembered to ring the police first it made no difference, for Dr. Buckthorne's car caught up Police Constable Beckett's bicycle and they arrived together. Warren was waiting for them at the main door and after a pause for an explanation more detailed than that provided over the telephone they made their way down to the swimming bath.

Watching the trio from his room, where he had gone for a tot of brandy, Begbie found himself bleakly reviewing the inevitable pattern of events that would follow. There would be an inquest; policemen would start asking questions; the school would get banner publicity. It was all most distasteful and his fastidious nature rebelled. Then, with a shock of horror at his own callousness, he realized he was thinking more of himself than of Carter. Remorse flooded over him and he wished he could take back every criticism he had ever made of the Head.

Now he had to go and teach as though nothing had happened; and somewhere, not far away, there was a cold-blooded murderer. He poured himself another brandy.

CHAPTER TEN

CHIEF DETECTIVE INSPECTOR BARNABY was not at all pleased to find himself on the 12:30 from Paddington to Weymouth. He had already postponed a fishing holiday in Ireland once, and now, with the end of the Duinish murder in sight, he had been relieved of the final knot-tying—and probably the kudos as well—and was being forced to put it off again.

His ill-temper was in no way allayed by the realization that Scotland Yard, in his person, was only on the new case as a result of skilled string-pulling. There had been a bare ten minutes for briefing on the Claydon affair before he had dashed to Paddington, but he gathered that a well-connected school governor, lacking confidence in the County C.I.D. and fearing the publicity of a protracted investigation, had exerted influence to have the Yard called in immediately. Barnaby's private disappointment was backed by public-spirited disapproval. What was more, he had been rushed off his feet as if he were a mere beat-pounding constable.

The case had its interest, he grudgingly admitted. Headmasters were not assassinated every day—which was strange, really, for they were obvious victims from several

points of view. He wondered what had been wrong with this
one. Sadist? Martinet? Or had he been seducing staff wives?
The body had apparently been found in the swimming pool.
Perhaps he had made a cold swim before breakfast
compulsory? He might as well think about something else
while he still had the leisure to do so. Why, for example, did
an express train for Weymouth go through Somerset at all?
And what was that curious grinding noise rising from the
entrails of the carriage which suggested that all was not well
with something rather important?

He appeared to be the only passenger who got out at
Frome and the bulky figure standing at one end of the
platform immediately approached and stiffly introduced
himself. "Sergeant Graham, sir. I've been appointed to
assist you with the Claydon Prior investigation."

Barnaby's spirit drooped when he heard the trade jargon,
but he approved the firm jaw-line, the humorous creases
radiating from the corners of the eyes, and the unmmistak-
able West-country accent.

Graham, for his part, at sight of the inspector, was
immediately reminded of the top-heavy matchstick figures
he had drawn in his books at school. For Barnaby was a tall
man, well over six feet, and his height was accentuated by
his lack of flesh. The immpression he created was entirely
one of bone and his clothes hung limply from the angles of
his body. No man of his build could ever be graceful and
when he walked down the platform his different members
jerked mechanically like those of a puppet. His face was
gaunt, yet somehow bright and inquisitive, and his eyes
were constantly on the move, suggesting continuous com-
bustion of nervous energy.

Barnaby only grunted to reply to Graham's formal
attempts at conversation. He did not speak until he had
levered himself awkwardly into the back seat of the police

car waiting in the station yard. Then he said: "How long does it take to get to this place?"

"About an hour, sir, if we don't hurry. Of course we can do it in much less if you give the word." Graham took care not to relax too completely beside his superior.

"No, an hour's peaceful drive will suit me. You can tell me what's happened here while I look at the countryside."

"Well, sir, I'm not sure that I know much more than you do. I've been up to the school, of course, just to get the hang of the place, but I couldn't stay long as I had to get here to meet you."

"Who's been in charge so far?"

"Inspector Singleton of the County C.I.D. He's up at the school now, but he knows he's only holding the fort until you arrive."

"I suppose he's sore about that?" Barnaby believed in being blunt.

"I don't think so, sir. To tell the truth the County's a bit stretched at the moment. A body was found in a packing-case at Yeovil Station last night and the inspector's going on to that."

"Brutal county; primitive instincts, I suppose," Barnaby mumbled to himself. To Graham he said: "I see. Well, just give me a summary of this case as far as you can, will you? All I know is that a headmaster has been found in a swimming pool."

"Yes, sir. Well, the local police—"

"Vandalism," said Barnaby quietly.

"I beg your pardon, sir?"

"Vandalism—sheer bloody vandalism."

Graham was nonplussed. Carefully arranging his narrative in textbook fashion, he found the interruption confusing.

"Look at those trees, Sergeant."

"Yes, sir." Obediently Graham looked out across the low wall of a sizeable country estate. A few unremarkable trees were dotted about in the park.

"When I was last on this road about two years ago, that park was full of most beautiful trees. Look at it now. They've cut down anything of size and left those few puny things. It's ruined. When they've pulled up the hedges as well—and they're bound to—the place will be a desert in ten years." He sat back suddenly. "Go on."

Graham struggled to make the necessary mental adjustment. "Well, the local police, sir—that is, Police Constable Beckett—he looks after Claydon Prior and Claydon Magna—well, Beckett was called to the school at 9:15 this morning. A private boarding school, you understand, sir. I believe—"

"Was this when the body was found?"

"Yes, sir. I gather a boy found it and they went down to see for themselves before ringing Beckett."

"They?"

"Two masters. A Mr. Warren and a Mr. Begbie. Warren's the deputy headmaster. Beckett arrived and found that the body had been pulled out of the pool. Carter—that's the Head's name—had been dead some while. Dr. Buckthorne—he's the local G.P.—puts the time of death between 8 and 10 last night. And unless the post-mortem shows up something else, it looks as though he was killed by a stab wound in the back."

"Weapon?"

"Nothing found yet, sir, but there are hundreds of places to look. Inspector Singleton was arranging for prints and photographs when I was up there."

Barnaby grunted, an ambiguous sound which Graham found hard to identify as favorable or otherwise. "How's the school taking it?"

"No sign of panic, sir. The masters are obviously shaken, but it's difficult to tell with the boys. My impression was that Mr. Warren had got most things under control." Graham paused, then leaned forward almost confidentially. "To tell the truth, sir, I don't know much about private schools. This one seems like a little world of its own and it's difficult to get on the inside."

"Quite right, Sergeant. Good observation. There's nothing quite so insular as a prep. school—that's all part of the system. They usually turn a tough shell of indifference to the everyday world around them, but this murder will get under their guard. It ought to be rather interesting."

For the first time Barnaby felt a twinge of almost pleasurable anticipation and relapsed into silence until the car slowed and turned into a drive between two red-brick pillars, each surmounted by a heraldic beast of great ugliness.

"Good Lord, what horrors!" he exclaimed, sitting forward abruptly; then, in the same breath: "When we get there, I shall speak to Singleton before he goes. After that I shall want to see the body—you'd better come too."

The car bumped in a couple of pot-holes in the ill-kept tarmac, turned a sharp bend, and the school, its red brick softened by the afternoon sun, swung into view beyond the cricket field. Seconds later, with a crunch of small stones beneath the tires, and with many pairs of eyes peering at it from hidden vantage points, the car stopped before the Gothic front door.

Singleton and Warren were on hand to meet it. Barnaby shook hands perfunctorily, then said to Warren: "I want to see the body first. Perhaps I could see you immediately afterward?" His manner was curt, almost rude.

Warren was not flustered. "Of course, Inspector. Sergeant Graham knows where my room is. I shall be available as soon as you want me."

"A cool customer," thought Barnaby, eyeing Warren's retreating gown. He turned to Singleton. "No doubt you want to get away, Inspector. I understand you have a gruesome package waiting for you at Yeovil. Just let me know how things have gone here and you can be off."

Singleton was a man of few words, but they were well-chosen ones so he covered the ground swiftly. Everything pointed, he suggested, to the fact that Carter had been killed while pouring chlorine into the swimming pool. A broken jug had been found at the edge of the pool and it looked as though he had dropped it when attacked. As yet no weapon had been found, though it was clear that the Head had been stabbed in the back with a knife of some sort. Dr. Buckthorne's estimate of time of death—somewhere between eight and ten—had been confirmed by the divisional police surgeon. The latter added that, if pressed, he would say the hour between eight-thirty and nine-thirty was the most likely.

Brief interviews with the staff had been unproductive. Although he gathered that Carter had not been popular, there was no obvious motive. The only person who stood to gain financially was Carter's middle-aged sister, his sole living relation as far as could be discovered, whose home was in Ireland and who had not seen her brother for more than six years. Anyway he had left barely £2,000. The one person who had said anything of interest was Gregg, the voluble gardener. He claimed to have seen somebody running from the swimming pool late the previous evening, but Singleton would not vouch for his trustowrthiness as a witness. "A good imagination and poor eyesight," he said gloomily.

Barnaby thanked him and Singleton took his leave, clearly delighted to be away from a case which offered no obvious lines of attack. Barnaby and Graham set off to view the body. They rounded the west wing of the school and turned toward a converted barn near the old stables. A bored-looking constable was standing at the door. Barnaby peered down at him disapprovingly, grunted, and then turned into the gym to inspect the lifeless thing lying on the trestle table usually used for cricket teas. Graham stayed outside. He had known death before, but did not choose to face it more than was necessary.

Ten minutes later the inspector reappeared. He held a small piece of material between thumb and forefinger. Graham recognized it as being from Carter's suit.

"Put this in an envelope, Sergeant. Then, as soon as you've shown me to Mr. Warren's room, have it taken to Bristol. I want to know what the splashes on it are. The car can take it, but make sure my case is left behind here. I don't want to have to sleep in my pants. The body can go, too," went on Barnaby, "but wait till the boys are in bed. The quicker we get the post mortem report the better. Then while I start on the masters I want you to chase up the kitchen staff, cleaners, and so on. Find out who they are, where they live, and what their movements were yesterday. And pick up any gossip there may be—that can be useful in a case like this."

Graham showed Barnaby up to Warren's room, then left on his mission with the bit of material. It was still wet; the spots to which the inspector had referred were only indistinctly visible. "He's got a good pair of eyes," was his unspoken tribute.

The excitement and disorder of the day's events had inevitably unsettled the boys, so most of the staff, themselves confused, had solved the problem by setting a great deal of written work. The result was an excess of marking, and Warren was ploughing through a pile of 'unseens' when Barnaby interrupted him.

"Please sit down, Inspector."

Barnaby lowered himself untidily into an armchair and started to speak before he had completed the process. "I'm sorry to trouble you, Mr. Warren, but I'm sure you will understand that I shall have a lot of questions to ask and I must start at the top. I believe you've been here longer than anyone else, haven't you?"

"I suppose I have, though Mrs. Quail—she's the matron—runs me close."

"What's happening about the school?"

"The Governors have appointed me temporary Head master until the end of term. We shall carry on as normally as possible." Warren, his gaze steady, looked back into the pale blue eyes so obviously appraising him. Unconsciously he had adopted the clipped verbal style of his interrogator.

"Good. The more normal the routine is, the easier my job will be. Now to business. I don't want an account of your own personal activities—that will come later—but I should like a review of events from about eight o'clock last night up to the finding of the body this morning."

"I'll do by best. How would you like it to start?"

"Do you know who last saw Carter alive?"

"Well, I last saw him after evening prayers—that would be about 7:45. But one of the kitchen maids served his supper and apparently he was all right then."

"What time was that?"

"I don't know for sure. He usually started his supper at about eight, but I haven't asked the girl about times."

"Did anybody else see him after that?"

"I can't say definitely, but we've been talking about it today, of course, and no one seems to have seen him after Mary—Mary's the maid."

"When was he first missed this morning?"

"At breakfast. Gregory—he's the Maths master, new this term—expected him to turn up to say grace as he always did. He waited a bit then said it himself, assuming Carter must have overslept. He'd done so once or twice before."

"And then?"

"Then he wasn't in morning assembly and we knew something was wrong. That was his peak performance of the day."

Warren made no attempts to hide the note of sarcasm in his voice. Barnaby made no comment. He was not after the personal view—not yet anyway. Quietly he said: "Please go on."

"Well, the discipline has been going haywire recently and a lot of boys have been skipping prayers. One of them, a young one called Donovan, was going to hide in the swimming pool enclosure, but he got a shock. Apparently he'd been in there several minutes before he realized what was in the water. He'd climbed over the fence to get in but he was so terrified, poor child, that he could hardly summon the strength to get out."

"What do the other boys know?"

"It was no use hiding too much. I told them there had been an accident and that the Head was dead."

"How did they take it?"

"It was a sharp jolt. Death is very remote to a boy; it doesn't come within his ken. They were shocked into silence for the first half of the day, but a reaction set in later."

"I suppose you got in touch with the Governors immediately?"

"Yes—I phoned the chairman, Lord Brisham. He lives about five miles away at Horton Gibbet. He came straight over and I suspect he had something to do with your swift arrival. He knows a lot of influential people."

"Apparently," said Barnaby dryly, scribbling a final note on the pad he had produced. "Good. I think that's all I want to know for the present. I expect the staff are getting restive at being confined, Mr. Warren. I had better see them soon. Could we manage 7:30, do you think?"

"Yes, I'll arrange that, Inspector. I'll get them all together in the staff room—that's the door on the left at the bottom of the stairs outside my door."

"Thank you—Oh, just one thing more. I shall need a room to work in where I shall be undisturbed."

"You can have Carter's study. Shall I show you where it is now?"

"No, later will be all right. I want to walk about and get the feel of the place before I meet the rest of the staff." Barnaby placed two horny hands on the two knees projecting before him and pulled himself upright. "Thank you, Mr. Warren, for being so helpful."

Warren, himself used to giving orders and having them obeyed, was impressed by the inspector's opening performance. There was a directness about his manner which suggested efficiency and his eyes were disquietingly penetrating. "He stands a good chance of getting to the bottom of this," Warren reflected. "But he's a very funny shape indeed."

CHAPTER ELEVEN

BARNABY made his way downstairs and looked hopefully around for a boy. He found two studying a notice-board in an area that was plainly one of the main thoroughfares of the school. "Hullo," he said.

The older of the boys, suddenly conscious of his own insignificant proportions compared with those of the giant looming over him, replied timidly, "Hullo," the added "sir" as an afterthought.

"What are your names?" Barnaby tried to look avuncular, and failed miserably.

"Clatworthy, sir. Clatworthy major. This is Clatworthy minor." He pointed disparagingly at the smaller boy. "Are you a detective?"

"As a matter of fact I am. Detective Inspector Barnaby."

Woodenly but correctly the elder Clatworthy held out his hand. "How do you do, Inspector." The younger boy took one sidelong glance at Barnaby and fled; the clatter of his feet on the tiles echoed as he vanished down the corridor. "Don't worry about Clatworthy mi., sir. The juniors are a bit upset about this business."

Barnaby did not know whether to be more astonished at the boy's aplomb or the fact that he referred to his brother by his surname. "Anything interesting on the board?" he asked, eyeing the green baize and the litter of notices.

"Not really, sir. Only one of the Rab—er—Mr. Warren's saying that discipline is going to be tightened up."

"Is that a good thing?"

The small brow puckered. Its owner gave a considered opinion. "Yes, I think so, sir. You see, Mr. Carter wasn't a very good headmaster. I'm sorry he's dead though."

Barnaby was unused to such frankness, but recognized a valuable source of information when he found one. "I want to go to the swimming pool. Will you show me the way?"

"Of course, sir. I'll take you by a short cut." Clatworthy, who relished the role of police confidant, quickly became voluble. Barnaby only had to direct the flow.

"What was wrong with Mr. Carter?"

Again the frown and studied reply. "Oh, I think he just didn't understand boys." He paused, trying to give his scattered ideas some semblance of coherence. "He never told anybody off properly, sir. You didn't know where you were. It's much easier when people say 'No' and mean it. He was always giving you another chance, however bad you'd been."

They turned into a narrow, dark corridor. It was cool there and damp patches scarred the ill-decorated walls. "This is out of bounds really, but it will be all right as I'm with you, sir." At the end of the passage they emerged into sunlight at the side of the school. "The pool is over there, sir, in the dip beyond the copse. We can go through the kitchen garden."

Barnaby looked at his watch. Automatically he was beginning to check times. They set off along a weed-strewn gravel footpath.

Just before they reached the trees, they came upon a

bonfire with an elderly man tending it. He straightened himself slowly and wiped his forehead with the back of his arm.

"Good evening. You must be Gregg, the gardener. Inspector Singleton was telling me about you."

"That's it, sir. My name's Gregg. I suppose you're the gentleman from Scotland Yard. I 'eard you'd arrived. But you'll 'ave to speak up, sir, because I'm 'ard of 'earing."

Singleton had said that Gregg was over seventy, but he did not look it. His face was brown with long days in the open air, a ruddy brown that spread down his neck and over his bald head; his voice was soft, tinged with the more agreeable elements of the Somerset accent; only his slow, thoughtful movements revealed his resignation to the passage of years.

"I shall have to ask you some questions, Gregg, later this evening. What time do you finish work?"

"No special time, sir. I've a lot to do at this time of year, bein' single 'anded, y'see. I don't suppose I shall finish before eight tonight. It were after nine last night that I called it a day. That's why I saw what I did," he ended significantly.

"Good," said Barnaby briefly, "I'll send for you when I want you. Then you can tell me everything in your own way."

Barnaby and Clatworthy continued toward the pool, the boy already mentally composing, and embroidering, the account of his experiences.

"How long have you been here?" asked Barnaby.

"Four years, sir. And this last year, since Mr. Carter's been Head, has been the worst. There's been no life in the school. Even the football team was rotten this year."

"What are the other masters like?"

"Oh, they're all right—some of them, anyway," was the

unenthusiastic reply. Clatworthy was not interested in the masters. "Have you found any clues yet?"

"One or two."

"Did Mrs. Quail do it, sir?" he asked hopefully. "She slippered me last night and she didn't half lay it on. It would be jolly good if you caught her." A glow of pleasure suffused his cheeks at the prospect.

They topped the last rise and the inspector dismissed his guide as soon as he had pointed out the door in the swimming pool enclosure. He had exhausted that front of information for the time being.

He arrived at the door on his own and found it locked. He shouted, and after a moment or two a red-faced Constable Beckett appeared. "Very sorry, sir," he apologized. "I locked it so that nobody could nip in behind me while I was searching inside. The bath's been put out of bounds, but you know what boys are."

"Fortunately I don't," rejoined Barnaby crisply. He went in and stood for a moment looking at the pool. Beckett, very much in awe of his superior from London, waited exectantly. He was patently anxious to please.

"Has anything been moved?"

"No, sir—not to my knowledge. Apart from the body, that is. It was down there." He pointed to the edge of the pool where a crude figure had been chalked on the flagstones.

"Any sign of the weapon yet?"

"No, sir. I've hunted high and low in here. The pavilion's the only place I'm not certain of. It's crammed full of junk and I could still be here tomorrow and not have searched it properly. I was in there when you shouted just now."

Barnaby walked down to the water's edge; Beckett followed at a discreet distance. "Now you were the first here this morning, Constable. Were these bits of broken jug exactly where they are now?" He stooped over the broken pieces.

"Yes, sir. Inspector Singleton had a look at them all, but he put them back for you to see. The handle has Carter's prints on it, so it does look as though he was carrying it when he was attacked, doesn't it, sir?"

Barnaby looked at the yellow-green chlorine that had splashed in all directions. "Yes, I think it does." Slowly he uncoiled himself; then, when he had reassumed the upright position, he jerked into motion and carried out a lightning survey of the grassy banks surrounding the pool. Beckett, fascinated like others before him by the action of his superior's limbs, followed his wake and hoped that he had not missed anything which the inspector would spot immediately.

The grass yielded nothing. Barnaby turned his attention to the pavilion. This was a ramshackle structure which had been thrown together at negligible cost when it was realized that the pool itself was to provide a bill substantially in excess of the original optimistic estimate. It had two sections. One contained some battered deck-chairs, a notice which proclaimed that they were for staff use only, and a series of clothes pegs, on which were suspended a nameless pair of trunks and an indescribably filthy towel belonging to Miller minor. The second room was more interesting and would have been a valuable piece of evidence for anyone studying the psychology of groundsmen. It was the most glorious of glory-holes, a microcosm of the junk-sheds of the world. A rough bench, scarcely visible under the variety of oddments beneath which it groaned, ran the length of one wall; the other walls boasted shelves, each crowded with paint tins, jam jars, flower pots of all shapes and sizes, and innumerable wooden boxes. Above the shelves, dangling from enormous nails like dead birds, were gardening tools, ranging from a rusty scythe without a handle to a bent-pronged fork on which, mildewed and shriveled, an ancient Arran Pilot was miserably impaled. The floor had not escaped. Two sacks bulging with mysterious contents dominated one corner; the chlorine jar, thrusting its glass head above the disorder, ruled the one opposite; elsewhere the litter of nails, bits of string and discarded football bladders ensured that it was impossible to move without treading on something different with each step. In short, it was the indispensable sort of shed into which everything is thrown and which, as a result, contains anything one may require on even the most unlikely occasion as long as one has the time to search for it.

Barnaby blenched. "This will keep you busy, Beckett. Turn the whole place upside down. If you don't find anything, we'll start a systematic search of the grounds tomorrow. But finish this tonight. I want that weapon."

With this melodramatic order, striking a note he reserved for junior constables, Barnaby turned and set off back to the main school buildings. So rapidly did he walk that he was already out of earshot when Beckett said, "Right, sir."

By 7:30 the masters were assembled in the staff room waiting for Barnaby. They had absorbed the shock of Carter's death in their individual ways, but now they were uniformly apprehensive. By common consent they avoided the problem of who might have been responsible for the situation; accordingly they thought about it all the more.

Barnaby knocked briefly and the already hushed voices faded as he came into the room. Jordon started to get up, but was waved down. "Stay seated, gentlemen, please."

The inspector's eyes glanced over the nervous faces before him. For a moment he ignored the chair Warren proffered. "Where are the matrons?" he asked.

There was a slight pause before Warren answered, "I

didn't ask them to come, Inspector. I didn't know you wanted them. Of course, I will send for them if you wish."

"Yes, please. Sergeant Graham is interviewing most of the domestic staff, but I think the matrons should be here."

There was an awkward silence while Mrs. Quail and Linda Grant were fetched, a silence which Barnaby did nothing to break. Once they had arrived, he formally addressed the expectant faces ringing the perimeter of the room.

"My name is Barnaby ladies and gentlemen. I must apologize for the inconvenience I shall be causing, but I'm sure you will understand that it's inevitable. The more cooperation I get, the quicker the whole affair will be cleared up. I know that Inspector Singleton asked some questions this morning and he has, of course, passed that information on to me. But I want you to regard me as starting from scratch."

He paused for breth and several heads nodded. He went on: "You all know, I'm sure, that there is little doubt that your headmaster was murdered last night." Each pair of eyes was lowered as Barnaby flicked his glance around. "There are four possibilities. One: he was killed by an outsider. Two: one of the domestic staff was responsible. Three: one of the boys did it. Four—"—there was an audible creak as someone stirred in his chair—"Four: one of you did it."

There it was, blunt and to the point: the simple statement of obvious fact which all had realized but which none had been brave enough to put into words throughout the long day. Maitland looked at Linda Grant. She was staring out of the window, her lips parted. Begbie uncrossed his legs and recrossed them, carefully avoiding looking at Barnaby. Gregory adjusted his spectacles with exaggerated care and blinked through them. Warren, usually firm and command-

ing, seemed somehow reduced in stature; he looekd at his
feet. Jordon was under the most obvious emotional stress:
his face was white and his hands twisted in his lap. Mrs.
Quail seemed least affected by the strangely taut personality
dominating the room; she stared stonily back into Barnaby's
chill blue eyes.

"A badly frightened lot," thought Barnaby. Aloud he
said: "Mr. Warren, as temporary Headmaster, has promised
his full support. I'm taking over Mr. Carter's private study
and I shall want to see you all individually this evening. I
shall be grateful if you will stay in the school until I say
otherwise."

Jordon tensed himself, hunched forward nervously in his
chair, and said: "Excuse me, Inspector, I—I'm married and
I live at the Lodge. May I go home?" He sounded like a
small boy asking for leave to go to the village.

"I should like you to wait until I've interviewed you, if
you don't mind. But, of course, you will be at liberty to go
home immediately after that."

"Very well, Inspector." Jordon sat back meekly, looking
exhausted.

"In the meantime, ladies and gentlemen"—Barnaby
contrived to continue as though he had not been interrupted—"the school should run as normally as possible."

He had apparently finished and was turning to the door
when an afterthought appeared to occur to him. "Oh, just
one thing," he said casually. "It's pretty clear that Mr.
Carter was killed while he was pouring chlorine into the
pool. I think it likely that whoever did the murder will have
traces of chlorine on his clothes, even it it's not immediately
visible. I tell you this because I shall want to go through
your wardrobes tomorrow, and if you've noticed unusual
stains on anyone's clothes you should let me know."

Again he turned for the door. This time he was halted by a brisk knock. "Come in," he said.

Police Constable Beckett came in. He stood stiffly for a moment, abashed at finding himself the center of attention. But his confidence returned as he looked at his superior. Tact and a sketchy police training went to the winds. "I've found it, sir. I'm sure I've found it."

Beckett held out his arm. In his hand he gripped a boy's sheath-knife.

Barnaby, overcoming his annoyance at this blundering revelation, sought to turn it to advantage by witnessing its effect. He spun around.

With one exception, all mouths had dropped open, all eyes were wide with surprise. The exception was Jordon. He had buried his face in his hands.

CHAPTER TWELVE

WARREN showed Barnaby and Beckett up to Carter's study, a comfortable book-lined roof that overlooked the cricket field. "Here we are, Inspector. I don't think there is anything in here that I shall have to trouble you for. All the papers for the general administration of the school are in the office. The Headmaster's secretary, Mrs. Greenish, is taking all incoming telephone calls, so you won't be bothered with them. She usually goes at five, but she's staying on tonight to cope with the crisis. The telephone has been red-hot today with parents and the Press ringing up to find out what's going on."

"Thank you, Mr. Warren. This will be admirable. Now I'd like to see the staff individually in a moment. Perhaps you would care to come first?"

"Certainly, Inspector. Just send for me when you're ready. In the meantime I'll go and see how prep. is going on."

Barnaby sat down in the large swivel chair behind the desk and turned to face Beckett, who was waiting expectantly by the window. "Congratulations, Constable. Where was it?" He took the knife, still wrapped in a handkerchief, and laid it on the desk.

"In the chlorine bottle, sir. I looked in soon after you'd gone and there it was. I suppose there's no doubt about it, sir?"

"Hardly any. It fits the doctor's specifications and the mere fact that it had been hidden in the jar shows somebody wanted to get rid of it. We'll have it tested for fingerprints, and the jar too, but I'm not hopeful." He paused. "Are you married, Beckett?"

"Yes, sir."

"Better ring your wife and tell her not to wait up—you'll be here some time. And have my case taken down to the pub in the village, will you? Sergeant Graham and I have rooms booked there. Tell them we'll be in late."

Beckett retired and Graham arrived before he could shut the door.

"Come in, Graham, and sit down. Anything from the domestics?"

"Not really, sir. I think we can rule most of them out if they're telling the truth."

"Good. It helps clear the ground. Tell me about them."

"Well, in the first place, sir, none of them lives in and all except two claim they were off the premises before eight last night. There are seven of them altogether, including Gregg, the gardener-cum-handyman. Three of them are part-time cleaners who come in to do rough chores and help with the washing-up. They only stay until four-thirty in the afternoon. I haven't seen them yet, but the others say their routine was the same yesterday. That leaves Mrs. Greaves—she's the cook—two maids, who live in the village, and Gregg."

"Yes, I've met Gregg. Where does he live?"

"Claydon Magna. And by all accounts, including his own, he was up here till quite late last night."

"So I gathered. We'll see him shortly. What about the cook?"

"She stays until about 6:30 p.m. to prepare high tea for the boys and the staff. She leaves it all ready and catches a bus to Shepton Mallet at 6:45 p.m. Oh, and while I think of it, sir, she says there's some cold supper for us in the kitchen if we care to collect it for ourselves later on. She stayed on to speak to us, but I've said she can catch the next bus home."

"She sounds a sensible body."

"She is, sir. Though no one thinks much of her cooking, I understand. That brings us to the maids—a middle-aged woman, Mrs. Crowther, and a girl of about twenty called Mary Croft. The normal procedure is for one to go off early while the other stays on to serve the Head's supper. It was Croft's turn to do the late duty last night and she swears Carter was alive and kicking when she served his prunes and custard at 8:35 p.m."

Barnaby pulled a face.

"She says she took the food in, said goodnight, and went straight home. She particularly noticed the time because she wanted to knock off."

"So she and Gregg are the only ones who were up here. What's she like?"

"Very pretty, sir—first-class figure. Knows how to dress, too. It's a good thing this is only a prep. school, sir, if you ask me."

Barnaby looked faintly sympathetic for the first time since his arrival. "What I meant, Sergeant, was, does she seem honest?"

"Yes, sir, I think so. She's a bit scatter-brained, I should say, and too interested in men. But she's probably telling the truth."

"Did you pick up any gossip?"

"A little, sir. No one liked Mr. Carter apparently. He seems to have rubbed them all up the wrong way. Rumor has it that he and Warren had been loggerheads for some time. And there's a strong hint of something going on between Mr. Maitland and Miss Grant. Mrs. Greaves was very disapproving."

"Well done. We've made a start. Now where's Beckett got to?"

Barnaby stood up, dug his hands deep into his pockets, and looked out of the window. An ambulance was moving slowly down the drive, followed by a police car. "The earthly remains of Henry Carter . . . Hullo, who's this?" A plum-colored Rolls-Royce had also appeared in the drive, heading in the opposite direction. It drove on to the grass to avoid the small cortège, then swung smoothly around to the front of the school and stopped outside the main entrance. The chauffeur opened the door for a brown-suited man with a shooting stick and a shapeless fishing hat.

"Trouble," said Barnaby. "If I mistake me not, this is Lord Brisham coming to throw his weight about. Probably wants to know why we haven't got it all sorted out by now. I suppose I must be diplomatic."

Graham said nothing. He did not yet know Barnaby well enough to be other than embarrassed by such comments about a social superior.

"I shall have to see him, Graham. Go and tell Mr. Warren there'll be a delay before we see the staff—and try and find out where Beckett's got to, will you?"

Graham departed and shortly afterward Beckett himself returned and announced Lord Brisham.

Brisham was large and untidy, with a grizzled mustache,

receding hair, and a shabby but well-cut tweed suit. A genial but fundamentally unintelligent man, he had remained insulated against the twentieth century by his insensitivity to changing attitudes around him. He thought of little but dogs, shotguns, keepers and fishing-rods, a world of illusion which he fortunately had the wealth to sustain. In short, he was an anachronism, harmless in himself but apt to try the patience of those with a job of work to do.

"How's it going, Barnaby? I've just seen Warren—a good man that—and he told me where to find you." He filled his pipe from an old leather pouch, scattering tobacco. "This has been a blow to the school, y'know. I hope it can be cleared up quickly, without fuss and all that."

"We've made a start. I shall be . . ."

"Was it a man from the village, or was it someone passin' through?" Brisham cut in with unintentional rudeness.

"As a matter of fact . . ."

"Come on now, Barnaby, there's no need to hedge with me, y'know. Nine times out of ten it's pretty clear which way the wind's blowing, isn't it? What's the picture here?"

Barnaby struggled with the metaphors, and to keep his temper. He was doing his best to humor the man because he saw little point in upsetting him, but he not suffer fools gladly and found those who asked questions and never waited to hear the answers particularly tiresome.

He tried again: "This is certainly not an obvious case, sir"—for the first time he inserted this courtesy—"but there's no evidence to suggest that Mr. Carter was killed by anyone *outside* the school. In fact . . ."

Brisham was not listening. "We made a mistake with Carter, y'know. He didn't go down well with the boys—or the parents for that matter. Too wishy-washy by half, and no grip—no grip at all. And now he's mucked it all up by getting himself killed by some lunatic. I suppose it was a lunatic? Must have been. Someone from outside the district—Bristol, I shouldn't wonder."

"In fact, all the evidence . . ."

"Evidence? Yes, that's what we need, Barnaby, evidence. I knew if we got the Yard in we'd get some evidence. Always go to the top, I say. No good relying on the local people. Very good in their way, I suppose, for traffic jams and all that, but when it comes to . . ."

Barnaby stood up sharply, his head thrust forward. "Lord Brisham, I do not wish to be rude, but I've had a tiring day and I've still got a lot to do here this evening. Now please listen to me. All the evidence points to a murderer *inside* the school. As yet I do now know who, but I promise you I'll find out and I'll do it with a minimum of publicity. I know you have the interests of the school at heart, but the best thing you can do is leave me in peace to get on with the job."

Brisham changed color: he became red, then white, finally he reverted to a blotchiness in which each of the various hues stood out vividly. Then, unexpectedly, he broke out into a genuine smile. "You're right, Barnaby, of course. I apologize—and I'll get out before I make a nuisance of myself." He stood up and exhaled a stream of acrid smoke. "Go straight to the top," he went on. "Get the best men, then leave them to it. You were quite right to tell me off. I'm an insufferable old boor." He smiled again.

"I beg your pardon, Lord Brisham. I . . ."

"Not another word. You put me in my place, and high time too. Do me good. You find the killer, then come and tell me about it. Come to dinner when it's all tied up. Bring your wife. Are you married? No? Nor am I—sensible fellow. Yes, come to dinner." He reached the door and extended his hand. Barnaby shook it. "You a fishin' man?

I've a nice piece of water at my place. Come and borrow a rod. Carter didn't fish, y'know. Didn't approve of what he called 'blood sports.' Funny man all around, but I don't suppose he could help it. No, we made a mistake choosin' him.''

The door closed. Barnaby sat down. "Silly old fossil," he said angrily, but he was not wholly insensitive to the underlying kindness of the man.

Graham and Beckett, who had been loitering in the corridor, reappeared immediately and Beckett was dispatched to fetch Warren.

Warren's account of the previous evening was concise and to the point. Though not entirely at ease, he maintained a cool detachment and seemed unmoved by the events he was describing. He had supervised prep. and had last seen Carter when he took prayers.

"Did you talk at all?" enquired Barnaby.

"Only platitudes about the weather and the swimming." Warren's tone suggested a mental shrug of the shoulders.

"Where did you go then?"

"I had a snack in the staff room, then went to my study and did some marking. After that, I suppose somewhere around nine o'clock, I went to see Begbie. We talked a lot, had a drink or two, and it must have been getting on for midnight when we eventually went to bed."

"Can you be more precise about times? When did you start marking?"

"Shortly after eight, I should think."

"Have you any means of proving you were in your room between eight and nine?"

"No, I don't think so." Warren spoke abruptly, as though unused to having his word doubted. "Oh, wait a moment. I had a telephone from a boy's father—a man called Browning. That must have been at about ten to nine. It was shortly before the end of the concert I was listening to on the wireless, and that ended at nine."

Barnaby asked about the concert and learned of the soloist's collapse. "Yes, a plucky effort, I thought," said Warren, taking the average concertgoer's view of a performance more notable for honest endeavor than artistic achievement. "She just managed to struggle on to the end and then the poor thing collapsed all over the keyboard. Nerves, I expect."

The last question was the only one to generate any emotion in Warren. "What did you think of Carter?"

"Hopeless," was the unhesitating reply. "Quite, quite hopeless. He's done his best to ruin an outstanding good school and even now it may be too late to repair the damage." He spoke with a new intensity and without further prompting from Barnaby gave a detailed account of the decline of the school and his own hostility to Carter.

"Ever seen that before?" asked Barnaby, pointing to the knife on the desk.

"We've tried to get rid of them, but there are still one or two around. No—I don't think I've seen that one."

Warren was released, with a request to send Begbie. Barnaby sent Beckett to check the Browning telephone call with the G.P.O.

Unlike Warren, Begbie had obviously been upset by Carter's death; his pallor still reflected the shock he had received earlier in the day. But his statement was clear enough. He had had an early supper to make sure he would hear the concert from the Festival Hall. It had started at eight and he had been in his room until the end. Warren had joined him shortly afterward and they had talked until midnight.

"I believe the soloist collapsed," probed Barnaby.

"Silly woman," replied Begbie. "Anna Kauper—she's

only nineteen, you know—fainted at the end of the third movement of the Brahms. Goodness only knows what made her choose it"—Begbie was relaxing visibly—"It's one of the longest in the repertory and needs real stamina. She was asking for trouble. Though I must say," he added sympathetically, "she wasn't at all bad in the first two movements. She won the Brovnik prize in Prague last year, you know."

"What happened after the concert?"

"There was a short 'fill-in' before a talk started at nine. John Warren came in soon after that and asked if I'd heard the girl collapse."

"You're sure he mentioned it first?"

"Yes—postive. He thought it amusing, I remember, and I couldn't see the joke. Anybody with a fancy central European name thinks he can come to England and get away with murder."

"What was the talk about—the one that started at nine?"

"I turned it off soon after Warren came in, but I think it was something to do with the history of place-names."

"And you spent the rest of the evening together?"

"Yes."

"I see. I don't think we need trouble you any more for the time being, Mr. Begbie. Perhaps you would ask Mr. Jordon to come up here in, shall we say, ten minutes' time?"

"Bit of a long-hair, if you ask me, sir," volunteered Graham, as the door closed. "Unreliable usually."

At this point Beckett returned with news of the telephone call. He confirmed everything Warren had said, or nearly everything. Warren had put the time at approximately ten to nine. The Post Office was more exact: it had been made at 8:40 and lasted four minutes.

"Well done, Beckett. Now I expect you and Sergeant Graham are hungry. Go down to the kitchen and bring up whatever the good Mrs. Greaves has left us. I want to finish all the preliminary interviews tonight, so we'll have it up here." To Graham he said: "We have a minute or two, so I'm just going to run over those two stories. Check my times with your notebook."

He glanced at his own notes on the desk, then stood up and began to pace around the room. "In the first place, unless they're in it together, neither of them could have done it at nine o'clock. They cover each other completely. Let's look at them before that. Take Warren. Two bits of information prove he was in his room at certain times; first, he says he heard the pianist collapse and secondly he had a telephone call. We've confirmed both of them. Begbie admitted that Warren mentioned the fainting fit first—ergo he actually heard it. And the G.P.O. supports the phone call."

"But not at the time Warren said, sir."

"That's true. But Warren was vague and didn't really commit himself. I doubt whether I could give you the time of a particular call to anything nearer than a quarter of an hour unless I had a very good reason for noting it.

"Now look at the times. Carter was still in his room at 8:35 p.m. if we believe the maid Croft. Even if Carter went down to the pool straight after supper, he couldn't have been there much before 8:50. It's a good ten minutes' walk—I've timed it. Then he had to get the jug and fill it with chlorine. So 8:55 looks like the earliest possible time for the murder unless we find something we don't know yet.

"But Warren was in his room talking to father Browning between 8:40 and 8:44, and he was still there when the girl collapsed. If you would just pass me that copy of the *Radio Times*, I'll check the times of the concert. Yes, here we are: 8 p.m. to 9 p.m. But you will remember that Begbie said there was a slight 'fill-in,' so it probably ended a few minutes early—say at about 8:57. So if Warren heard the collapse, and Begbie has proved that he did, he couldn't possibly have been killing Carter at 8:55, even if he sprinted both ways in gym shoes."

"But Begbie's not covered at all, sir."

"Yes, I know. But in my experience suspects with no alibi at all are usually innocent. I should be much more suspicious of Warren's story were it not for the fact that it is composed of a set of circumstances of which he could have no advanced knowledge and over which he had no control. After all, he has a motive of sorts."

The return of Beckett, bearing a tin tray piled high with sandwiches, cold sausages and fruit, broke up the dialogue. "I thought you and the Sergeant might be hungry, sir," he explained apologetically, "so I picked up a bit extra from the staff supper. They don't seem to have eaten much down there."

"Thank you, Constable. Put it on that chest by the window. We'll have it when we've seen the rest of the staff."

There was a tentative tap at the door.

"This will be Jordon," said Barnaby quietly. "Come in."

It was not Jordon, however. The door opened slowly to reveal Gregg, now wearing an old check jacket and looking older than he had done in the garden. "I think you ought to see me now," he said, " 'cos I've finished the beans and I'm off 'ome."

CHAPTER THIRTEEN

GREGG gave a perfect peformance. Bent, gnarled and weatherbeaten, he was exactly what every townsman expects a countryman to be. As a witness, he was at once infuriating and indispensable. The interview had to go at Gregg's pace and every attempt to speed him up ended in failure. Beckett was sent to delay Jordon.

At the end of twenty minutes Barnaby considered he had got what he wanted. From the mass of irrelevant detail and comment provided in Gregg's discursive survey, certain facts stood out.

Gregg had spent the previous evening preparing the cricket pitch in front of the school and had finally stopped work at nine. He had noticed the time because of a difference between the school and church clocks—a discrepancy which enabled him to launch an attack on the papel leanings of the new vicar. Within the crucial period he had noticed several movements. Fairly early on, certainly before eight, Miss Grant and a young teacher from the village school had walked down the drive; Miss Grant had returned alone. Later, probably at about 8:30, Mary Croft

had gone to the village across the fields; he thought he had
seen Mr. Maitland in the trees near the swimming pool at
about the same time, but he would not swear to it. Shortly
after that—pressed, he said about 8:45—he had seen Mr.
Carter walk down to the pool. He remembered it distinctly
because he hoped the Headmaster was not going to interfere
with the things in his shed. At two or three minutes to
nine—and here he was certain of the time because he had
been about to stop work—someone had run back to the
school along the path from the pool. He could not say who it
was because it was getting dark and the figure had been
running fast.

Barnaby was just assimilating this when he became aware
of a commotion in the entrails of the building. A door
banged noisily and a woman's shrill voice rose in anger.
Other voices, male and female, provided a garbled accom-
paniment in a lower register. Another door banged and it
was apparent that the disturbance, now recognizable as a
furious argument, was moving nearer. Its progres down the
final corridor was brisk. As the din reached a crescendo, the
door of the study burst open and a small yellow-haired
woman thrust herself into the room. Behind her, framed in
the doorway looking embarrassed, stood Maitland, Jordon,
and Mrs. Quail.

The policemen rose. Only Gregg seemed unconcerend.
"As I were saying," he went on, "there's more work 'ere
than's right for one man. I told Mr. Carter, I said . . ."

The shrill voice interrupted him; the yellow hair shook
with rage. "Who's in charge here? Is it you? Or you?" She
pointed accusingly at Barnaby and Graham.

"I am in charge of this investigation, madam," replied
Barnaby, summoning all his dignity and falling into the
jargon he deplored, "and I must ask you . . ."

"Well, listen to me." The rigid little figure swung around

with venom. "I don't know what you're playing at up here, but I've had enough of it. My husband was out all yesterday evening and came home stinking drunk and now I'm told he can't come home tonight until he's answered a lot of damn-fool questions. I've been slaving away in that filthy little Lodge all day. I've made his tea and cooked his supper—and what happens? Nothing! He might have been arrested for the murder for all I know. No one has told me anything. I might as well have been dead myself for all anyone cared. I . . ."

"Madam, I'm sorry you've been inconvenienced, but I fear a lot of people are put out when murder is committed. I hope . . ."

"Who cares about Carter?" was the scornful rejoinder. "No one here, I can tell you that. Good riddance, I say . . ." Her voice rose hysterically.

Behind her Maitland stepped forward. "Come now, Mrs. Jordon, Inspector Barnaby has a lot to do and he'll do it quicker if we get out of his way. He'll soon have finished with your husband."

Alice Jordon rounded on him. "You mind your own business. You've got enough to do chasing around after your women friends without poking your nose in where its not wanted. How far have you got with Linda Grant? She's got expectations, hasn't she, so perhaps you're after more than sex this time. It makes a change."

With Mrs. Jordon's attention once more on the knot of attendants who had tried to prevent her arrival, Barnaby seized the initiative. Planting a firm hand on her shoulder, he propelled her toward the door. "If you go back to the staff room for a short while, Mrs. Jordon, I'll see your husband immediately and he'll be free within ten minutes. I suggest"—he spoke over the yellow head in front of him in the direction of Mrs. Quail—"I suggest a little brandy might meet the case."

Still protesting, Mrs. Jordon retired, firmly shepherded by Mrs. Quail. Barnaby took advantage of the open door to shoot out Gregg, who had shown ominous signs of reembarking on his narrative. Jordon, who had said nothing throughout his wife's outburst, remained behind looking miserable.

"Please sit down, Mr. Jordon. I'll try not to keep you too long." Barnaby looked at him carefully but not unkindly. He had already seen the knife on his desk. "You recognize it?" Barnaby pointed nonchalantly with his pencil.

"I'm afraid so, Inspector. I confiscated it yesterday morning from a boy carving his name on a desk."

"When did you see it last?"

"Yesterday afternoon. I intended to put it in the confiscation box after lunch, but I'm a little absent-minded and I forgot. So I carried it about all afternoon and finally left it in the staff room at tea-time."

"Did anyone see you put it there?"

"Yes. Let me see, Maitland and Begbie were having tea at the time—but surely, Inpector, you don't imagine either of them is responsible?"

"Please don't jump to conclusions, Mr. Jordon. I suppose any member of the staff could have seen the knife if he had looked in the box?"

"Yes, I suppose so," Jordon agreed doubtfully.

There was something touching about the way Jordon, obviously worried about his own position, appeared genuinely concerned not to incriminate anyone else.

"Tell me about yesterday evening, Mr. Jordon."

"My wife was not wholly inaccurate, I fear, Inspector. I went to the De Mallet Arms for a drink."

"What time would that be?"

"Quite early. I think I was there by seven."

"When did you leave?"

"I'm not sure. I must admit, Inspector, that I drank more than was good for me and my recollection of events is a little hazy."

"Had you any special reason for doing so? Did anything unusual occur yesterday?"

The brisk barrage of questions pushed Jordon off balance. He drew a deep breath and looked Barnaby straight in the face for the first time. "No, Inspector. Nothing at all. It was a perfectly normal day." And Barnaby had the impression that he took more care over the enunciation of that sentence that anything else he said.

"You went straight home from the pub?"

"Yes, I think so. My wife wasn't very pleased—as you may imagine."

"Thank you for being so frank, Mr. Jordon. That will be all for the present. Would you ask Mr. Maitland to come up, please?"

"I'm sorry for that man, sir," said Graham, when Jordon had slipped unobtrusively from the room.

Barnaby grunted ambiguously. "All the same he's keeping something back."

Through the window the sky, blue and still quite innocent of cloud, was darkening as night came down. Barnaby swung his chair around and looked out at the hills dominating the valley. He glanced at his watch. "Half past eight," he mused aloud. "It's a pity we can't turn back the clock to this time last night. It would save us a lot of time and energy." Even as he spoke the blue took on a deeper shade; the hills were now merely etched in outline, all details on their surface had been obliterated. The last shadows in the park vanished; the trees down by the road rolled together like dark green clouds.

Barnaby suddenly sat erect. "Who's that?" he said sharply.

A figure, small and indistinct, had detached itself from the far end of the building and was setting off at a brisk trot across the cricket field toward the woods.

"That's Mr. Gregory, sir," said Beckett. "I suppose he's heard you want Maitland next and has taken the opportunity to go for a stroll."

"Perhaps. But he's not exactly strolling." Gregory had taken a diagonal line across the park and was following it undeviatingly. He reached a hedgerow, crossed it, took up the same route and then disappeared in a fold in the ground. "I think Mr. Gregory will have some explaining to do. I made it plain that I didn't want anyone to leave the building tonight."

Maitland arrived and sat down confidently. He smiled and offered his cigarette-case.

"No, thank you, Mr. Maitland, not just at the moment."

"Mind if I do?" He selected a cigarette with care, lit it with an expensive lighter, inhaled deeply and relaxed in his chair. "Go ahead, Inspector."

Maitland's air of self-assurance and outward calm did not deceive Barnaby for one moment; he had met the type too often. In fact, of all the people he had seen so far, Maitland had the least individuality.

"I would like you to think about yesterday evening, Mr. Maitland. What did you do from about eight o'clock onwards?"

"Well, I had my supper at about a quarter to eight and I suppose it must have been about a quarter past when I went out for a drive."

"Did anyone see you go?"

"I've really no idea, Inspector." Maitland smiled faintly. "I know what I see, but I can't account for other people. As a matter of fact, I should think it's a bit unlikely. I went out by the back entrance, which comes nowhere near the main buildings."

"Why?" asked Barnaby shortly.

"Why not?" shrugged Maitland. "It was the quickest way to where I was going."

"Where was that?"

"Oh, a little tour of the Mendips—Wells, Priddy, Shepton Mallet."

"Did you stop at all?"

"Yes, several times." His smile was now a confident grin. "The Blue Boy at Wells, the George at Morton Parva, and I think I finished up at the Barley Mow at Shepton."

"You're lucky I'm not investigating a case of drunken driving, Mr. Maitland. Were you drunk?"

"No, certainly not. I was cheerful, but nowhere near plastered."

"What time did you get back here?"

"About eleven-thirty, I should say, but I can't be sure. I was in the Barley Mow at closing time."

"Did you come in by the back entrance?"

"Yes, I did. I didn't want to wake the whole place up by using the main drive."

"Seen that before?" He pointed to the knife.

"Yes, old Jordon put it in the confiscation box yesterday at tea-time."

"Thank you very much, Mr. Maitland. That will do for tonight. Would you ask Mrs. Quail to come up next, please?"

The door closed; Graham and Beckett looked expectantly at Barnaby.

"Veneer of self-confidence," he said. "Not exactly my cup of tea. I don't want to be prejudiced against him, but I was interested in that woman Jordon's talk of 'expectations' from Linda Grant. That's the first mention of money in this case so far and in my experience it has more to do with murder than any other motive."

He relapsed into silence. His colleagues eyed the food by the window hungrily.

An authoritative knock announced Mrs. Quail.

CHAPTER FOURTEEN

MRS. QUAIL answered Barnaby's questions with a calm dignity that contrasted favorably with Maitland's exaggerated nonchalance. She sat quietly and confidently, radiating a repose all her predecessors had sought in vain.

No: she had not seen the knife before, nor did she believe any member of the staff could be responsible for Carter's death. Yes: she understood the Headmaster had been unpopular with the masters, but the inspector would understand that it was not her practice to discuss the Headmaster behind his back. What did she feel about his death? She was shocked, and she spoke as though the whole affair was an affront to the smooth routine of the school of which she was dedicated.

"How did you spend yesterday evening, Mrs. Quail?"

"I was on duty all the time as it was Miss Grant's half-day. The boys started coming upstairs in shifts from 7 p.m. onwards and I didn't leave the washrooms and dormitories until about 8:30 p.m., when all the boys were in bed. Then I went to my room to watch television and have a cup of coffee."

"And you stayed in your room until you went to bed?"

"Not exactly. I undressed at about 10:30 and was just washing when I was called to a boy who had been sick—a not infrequent occurrence. I went along to the dormitory to see it was nothing serious, put the child straight, and then went to bed. That must have been at about 10:45. I didn't leave my room until a quarter of seven this morning."

"Have you any proof that you were watching television between 8:30 and 10:30?"

"None at all," she said coldly.

"Miss Grant's room is on your floor, I believe. Was she in all the evening?"

"I really can't say, Inspector. Her room is a long way from mine and we're separated by the Cavalier and Roundhead dormitories. The dormitories have names," she explained.

"I see. Did you see any member of the staff at all once you had gone upstairs to put the boys to bed?"

"Yes, I saw someone going upstairs when I went to cope with the boy who was sick. I was in the dormitory at the time and the light on the stairs is only a dim one so I can't say who it was. I assumed it was one of the masters who has rooms up there—Mr. Warren, Mr. Maitland, Mr. Begbie, or Mr. Gregory."

"That must have been some time between 10:30 and 10:45?"

"Yes, Inspector."

"Have you heard any gossip about Miss Grant and Mr. Maitland, Mrs. Quail?"

Mrs. Quail was unmoved by the sudden change of direction. "I don't listen to gossip, Inspector."

She withdrew in good order. She had answered every question firmly and precisely; she had convinced Barnaby she was speaking the truth; and now she had gone, there remained the vacuum that people of strong character leave behind them.

"Not exactly the maternal type I should want for a son of mine if he had to go to boarding school," said Barnaby. "But a convincing witness."

"She has a reputation for being a dragon in the village, sir," said Beckett suddenly. "Mrs. Slater at the Post Office is terrified of her. And she's a prickly old termagant herself."

"She certainly put me in my place when I asked about gossip," admitted Barnaby.

Shortly afterward another knock sounded and Linda Grant came in. She sat down demurely and smiled at the three policemen. Barnaby's instinct told him the air of modesty was a little too calculated.

"How long have you been Assistant Matron here, Miss Grant?" asked Barnaby.

"Two years at the end of this term," she replied softly.

"Have you enjoyed it?"

This was obviously not the type of question she had been expecting. She tilted her head slightly to one side.

"On and off," she said. "The last year has been hard work. It's been an uphill struggle to keep the boys under control."

"Had you expected anything like this?"

"No, Inspector. I've heard several members of the staff swear at him at one time or another—but I expect you've sworn at people before now."

She smiled engagingly. Barnaby was not to be drawn.

"Maybe," he said dryly, "but I've not had to explain a murder afterward. Now, Miss Grant, I would like you to tell me in your own words exactly how you spent last evening."

"That's easy," said Linda, still smiling in spite of her rebuff, "because I hardly did anything at all. It was my half-day and I had a friend in for tea. Her name's Christine Bradby, and she teaches in the village. She stayed for an early supper as well and eventually went home at about a quarter to eight. I walked down to the end of the drive with her and then came back to my room."

"Did you go out again?"

"No. I was back in my room by about eight and I stayed there for the rest of the evening. I did a bit of washing and hung it out to dry on the balcony outside my room, but otherwise I was inside watching television and sewing. I went to bed quite early—at about ten."

"Did you see anyone between the time you saw your friend off and the time you went to bed? Could anyone—a boy perhaps?—prove that you were in your room?"

Linda thought for a moment, turning her head to look out of the window and showing her profile to advantage.

"No," she said at last. "I saw Mr. Gregory walking down the drive earlier in the evening. And I saw the light on in Mr. Begbie's room as I came back from seeing my friend off. But I don't think I saw anyone else."

"So you didn't see anything—or hear anything—which might help us? You didn't see, for instance"—he paused significantly—"Mr. Maitland?"

"No, Inspector," she replied quickly. "I didn't see anyone at all." She stared back at Barnaby, not confidently but with determination.

"Hit the mark with Maitland, sir," said Graham, when Linda Grant had gone to fetch Gregory.

"Yes, kitchen gossip is usually pretty reliable. I fancy there's something between them, but it doesn't necessarily help us. And nor do any of the other stories we've heard. All we've got so far is a pile of stuff that must be checked tomorrow."

They had not long to wait for Gregory.

"Sit down, please, Mr. Gregory," said Barnaby. "I'm sorry you've had to wait. But I have only a few questions to ask, so this will be quite brief."

"Thank you," said Gregory, sitting down primly and prodding his spectacles to the top of his nose with his forefinger.

"I understand this is your first term at Claydon, Mr. Gregory. This makes your evidence more valuable than most because you can be more objective. What is your impression of the school?"

Gregory did not reply immediately, his diffidence born of lack of confidence rather than loyalty to his colleagues. For all his advanced ideas he was overawed by the three policemen.

He looked up, blinking. "Not a good school, Inspector. The others say it was all right before Carter came, but I don't know whether to believe them. Their ideas are very traditional."

"I understand there has been some dissatisfaction. But had anything led you to believe that murder was possible?"

"No—I—well, yes. The atmosphere has been sour. It's difficult to pin down. There was tension—bitterness— somehow everybody was involved. Even I got caught up in it, and poor Jordon. It was . . ." Gregory struggled for words, though he knew he could not express ideas coherently which he had not fully grasped himself.

"Have you noticed anything particular which you think may have a bearing on what happened yesterday—anything at all?"

Gregory was about to say 'No,' when he remembered an odd incident at the beginning of term. Barnaby noticed his hesitation. "Anything at all, please, Mr. Gregory."

"There was one thing, Inspector. It was a day or two after the beginning of term. Mr. Carter was taking evening prayers after prep, as he always did. The duty master and duty matron sometimes attended as well and on this occasion they were Mr. Begbie and Mrs. Quail. I was there because I was new and was being shown the routine. Carter finished the prayers then, just as he was leaving, he tripped and dropped his books on the floor. Later, I realized it was typical of him—he was clumsy, always dropping things or knocking them over. Anyway, the boys tittered and Carter himself laughed. But I happened to look at Mrs. Quail and"—he hesitated—"and if ever I saw stark hatred it was on her face then."

Barnaby grunted characteristically and made a jotting on the pad in front of him. "Nothing else?"

"Well, yesterday evening I . . ."

"Wait a moment, Mr. Gregory," interrupted Barnaby. "If you're going to talk about yesterday evening, I'd like you to start at the beginning. Tell me everything you did."

"Right," said Gregory, whose confidence was increasing. "After tea I supervised a meeting of the boys' Chess Club. Then I had an early supper and went down to the pub for a drink—the De Mallet Arms, it's the only one. I had a drink or two and later on I heard Jordon in the other bar. He had drunk too much. I was surprised because I had no idea he drank at all. But shortly afterward, when I came out of the pub, I found him sitting on a bench crying his eyes out."

"Did you speak to him?"

"No." Gregory blushed. "I didn't want to get involved. In any case he didn't stay long. He got up and walked away up the High Street."

"What time was this?"

"It must have been about eight-thirty. I was back in the

school somewhere around nine, I did some marking, had a read, and was in bed by eleven."

"Did you see anybody from the time you left Jordon till the time you went to bed?"

There was a fractional hesitation, so brief that only a skilled interrogator would have noticed it. "Gregg was working on the field when I came up the drive, but I didn't see anyone else. I didn't leave my rooms once I'd got there."

Barnaby grunted again, then leaned forward. Graham recognized the danger signs.

"That deals with *last* night, Mr. Gregory. Now perhaps I could have an explanation of your behavior *this* evening." His manner, hitherto courteous and mild, was suddenly barbed. "What took you over the fields and down to the woods when I had told you to remain on hand?"

Gregory blinked; his confidence had evaporated. "Its hot in the staff room. I went out for a breath of air, just a short walk."

"You went nowhere in particular?"

"No."

"All right, Mr. Gregory—thank you."

He made a gauche and untidy exit.

"And yet you were running," said Barnaby quietly, "and you were following a very straight line."

"Now for some food," said Barnaby, leaning back in his chair.

There was a short period of silence while the three men started their belated supper. The inspector ate sparingly, closely examining each item before consigning it to his mouth; Beckett was tentative, making sure that he consumed neither more nor less than his superiors; Graham, unhampered by fears of appearing rustic, ate noisily and with evident relish.

"If we accept 8:30 to 10:00 as the critical time," mused Barnaby aloud, "they're practically all possibles, including the women. The doctor says either a man or woman could have produced the wound. Unfortunately there's a shortage of motive. They all disliked him, but no one seems to have hated him."

"Mrs. Quail?" hazarded Graham, brushing some prominent crumbs off his sleeve. "After all, Gregroy said . . ."

"Yes, there may be something there," cut in Barnaby impatiently, "if we scratch beneath the surface. And there may be a motive in the Maitland-Grant money angle. After all, Gregg thought he saw Maitland near the pool at about 8:30 and on Maitland's own admission no one was likely to have seen him drive off on his pub crawl, so he could have left later than he said. I'm certainly cautious over Grant: she lied at least once."

He paused, waiting for a cue.

Beckett obliged: "How do you know, sir?"

"Because she said she saw the light on in Begbie's room. Either she gave us the wrong time for the departure of her friend, which I doubt, or else she was outside at a later time and forgot exactly when she saw the light. Begbie would have no cause to put his light on before 8:15 at the earliest.

"She wasn't the only one lying either. Mrs. Quail said she saw someone on the stairs at about 10:30, but it doesn't tie up with any of the men who live above her. Warren and Begbie were together after 9:00. Gregory claims that he was in his room by approximately the same time, and Maitland was not back until 11:30. Of course, it could be Mrs. Quail lying, but if so, why?"

Neither Graham nor Beckett had the temerity to answer a

question that was plainly rhetorical, so Barnaby went on: "Then there's friend Gregory. He's an odd fish. On the surface a mild, insignificant little man—and I don't see how he can have worked up a motive in the short time he's been here. But his sortie down to the woods this evening still needs a satisfactory explanation. And I think he lied before, too. You remember when I asked if he'd seen anyone after leaving Jordon near the pub? I think he *did* see someone.

"As for Jordon, I'm tempted to believe most of his story, and frankly if I had a wife like his I'd take to drink too. Even so, he was obviously upset yesterday, and there's something he wants to conceal. He . . ."

The telephone rang peremptorily. While Barnaby held a brief and, for his part at least, monosyllabic conversation, Graham and Beckett cleared the remnants of food.

"Bristol," explained Barnaby laconically. "It was chlorine on Carter's suit, so unless our murderer is fiendishly clever we can rule out ideas of Carter being killed elsewhere and his body dumped afterward. He was almost certainly struck down while pouring the chlorine. That being so, I may have an interesting night ahead of me."

The others did not pick up this enigmatic remark. "What about Gregg, sir?" asked Beckett, as though there had been no interruption.

"Ah, yes—the voluble Gregg. I almost forgot him. He's rather like the postman in that Chesterton story. He's there all the time and merges so well with the scenery that no one notices him. He had the opportunity without a doubt, but I can't see a grain of motive—in fact, I can't see a motive anywhere."

He stood up abruptly. "Right, that's all for you tonight. I'll just see Warren to tell him I want to talk to the boys tomorrow. I'll meet you on the terrace at the front."

When he had arranged to address the boys at the nine o'clock assembly, he rejoined Graham and Beckett and together they made their way down the drive toward the village. As they walked, he outlined the programme for the next day.

"It will be tedious, but it can't be helped. Graham, I want the Maitland story checked—you can take the car. Beckett, you can have till eleven to deal with any routine business in the village, then I want you to cover the domestic staff again. We know what they say they did: I want each one checked. You can leave out the Croft girl—we'll deal with her. I shall be up at the school all the morning. It's time I went through Carter's papers."

Outside the gates, he stopped for a moment to get his bearings. The school building was invisible behind its protective belt of trees; the park itself was bathed in pale moonlight. The two beasts on the pillars at the entrance to the drive gained a new quality from the night: earlier they had been comic; now they were brutally alert.

"I'll come a bit further with you," said Barnaby suddenly. "I want to get back to the school unseen and I shall have more chance if I avoid the drive altogether. I fancy our quarry may make a move tonight and it would save a lot of trouble if I could catch him *in flagrante*, as it were."

He offered no further explanation and declined their offers of assistance. They turned down the lane toward the village, keeping the wall of the park on their left and, as the hedgerows were treeless, walking in the light of the moon. Five minutes' brisk progress brought a sharp bend in the lane before it dipped and plunged into the wood which spread on both sides.

The moment the trees closed overhead Barnaby pulled up

short. "This is as far as I'm coming. Make sure a door is left open for me at the pub, Graham, and you'd better leave a note telling me how to find my room. I hope I shan't be long. Goodnight to you both."

He crossed the ditch in front of the wall with one stride and levered himself through a breach where the stones had fallen away. He was back in the park.

CHAPTER FIFTEEN

ONCE over the wall and into the wood Barnaby paused, his senses suddenly sharpened now that he was alone. Behind him he heard the voices of his erstwhile companions and the fading crunch of their feet on the road; they were in step, he noticed. Ahead the trees, growing closely together and barely discernible in the darkness, effectively excluded the moonlight; only the faint glow fringing the leaves overhead hinted at the brighter world he had left. The air was still and cool.

Although he could see little, he had a good idea of his position. He was in the stretch of woodland bordering the school estate and he had only a short way to go before he came to the open park whence he should be able to see the main building; indeed, he had gone barely thirty yards when he became aware of a brightness ahead of him that marked the edge of the wood. He made toward it, picking his way between the trees and trying to avoid catching his clothes in the tangle of undergrowth that constantly clutched at him from the shadows. As the trees thinned and the moonlight at last filtered through, he increased speed and was soon gazing across the wide expanse of grassland separating him from the school.

It was going to be difficult to reach it without being seen. All the front windows commanded the ground over which he had to travel and the only cover was provided by a few fine oak trees, remnants of a more leisured age than either the school or its builder had known, and a low hedge running in a rough dog-leg line toward the cricket field. Barnaby began to regret he had not stuck to the tree-lined drive, or that he had not taken more trouble to approach from the rear. But he had no time to change his mind now; he must do the best he could with limited resources.

Accordingly, he moved back under the trees to get on the side of the hedge offering the most shade and then set off into the moonlight. At first he kept low, bending his untidy frame in an effort to keep it below the line of the hedge, but after a while he was delighted to find that as a result of the hot weather the ditch running parallel to the hedge had dried up and he could walk along it under full cover. He only hoped it went the whole length of the field and did not desert him halfway to his destination.

His luck held and shortly he found himself beneath the oak that stood over the little white cricket pavilion. Here the hedge and its accompanying ditch halted, so he paused to consider his next step. He slipped around to the back of the pavilion, inwardly smiling at the incongruity of a grown man creeping conspiratorially around corners which in the course of a normal day witnessed many a schoolboy melodrama, then cursed aloud and froze into immobility as he trod noisily on something metallic. Carefully he moved his feet, this time testing the ground before shifting his weight as he had once been taught in the army. He looked down and saw he had tripped over the pile of metal numbers used for the diminutive scoreboard hanging drunkenly on one side of the pavilion.

He was less that fifty yards from his destination now and these promised to be the most difficult. He looked up at the school, wondering at the crudity of its pseudo-Gothic design standing bared in the moonlight. But the futility of its heroic battlements was of only passing interest; his eyes shifted from the romantic turrets down to the lights still shining in five windows. Four of these were on the second floor: the men were still up. The other was more or less centrally placed on the first floor and even as he watched Mrs. Quail appeared and drew the curtains with two brisk motions. He was in good time; in fact, he might as well stay where he was for a while. He retreated and lowered himself to the ground.

He sat quite still for about ten minutes, then stirred as one of the top lights went out. Five minutes later another square of light vanished and was followed almost immediately by Mrs. Quail's. He stood up, stretched, and with his eyes fixed on the two lights still shining, swiftly crossed the intervening distance to the school. He took a second or two to recover his breath, then began to feel his way around the wing of the building. He wanted to find the door by which Clatworthy had taken him on the short cut to the swimming bath and for which he had appropriated from Carter's study a key labelled 'Disused Garden Door.' Here in the shadow there was little chance of being seen, but silence was important now and he advanced with the utmost care. He came on certain landmarks he remembered: a decayed greenhouse, leaning precariously; an abandoned wheelbarrow without a wheel; and over to the right, on the edge of the unkempt kitchen garden, the dull glow of Gregg's perpetual bonfire. The smell of burning hung in the calm air.

"And somewhere here," he thought, turning to the wall, "should be the door."

Yes: there it was, neglected and overgrown with ivy, the door he had been taken through earlier in the day. He stood still for a moment to listen, then, reassured by the silence, he unlocked it, turned the handle gingerly, and pushed. To his relief the door opened; to his surprise it did so comparatively quietly. He bent his head and went inside.

He was once more in the narrow, airless corridor, and a solitary ray of moonlight revealed the stained walls he had noticed earlier. He moved forward confidently for he remembered the passage was devoid of furniture; but he had forgotten three small steps which the moon failed to illumine and he fell to his knees as he stumbled clumsily up them. He swore softly. At the end of the passage he reached the hall containing the notice-boards and paused uncertainly. He wanted to make for the kitchen and there was a choice of four doors. He tried one and congratulated himself on his luck; the unmistakable smell of institutional cooking, an amalgam of overdone cabbage an other odors less easily defined, assured him he had chosen correctly. He pushed on and at the end of another corridor reached a well-equipped kitchen, clean, tidy, and obviously left for breakfast. A little too prepared, thought Barnaby, observing a pile of sliced bread apparently destined to become toast and already curling at the edges.

But he was interested in cookers, not toast, and he rounded the central table to look at the large Aga which dominated the far wall. On this all his hopes depended.

He knew the answer to his question before he reached it: the warm air surrounding the cooker plainly indicated that it was kept alight all night and a cursory inspection of the draught-regulator confirmed it with the tell-tale brightness of glowing coke. He was relieved; his first guess had been

right. Now all he could do was wait and hope—hope that
someone, he had no idea who, would think along the same
lines as himself. It was a remote chance, but in a case
offering so few leads anything was worth trying; at the
worst he would only lose a little sleep. So he picked up one
of the plain wooden chairs, put it in a concealed position on
the far side of a large cupboard and settled down to wait.

The first twenty minutes passed quickly. Eyes and ears
alert, Barnaby sat expectantly on the edge of his chair. But
the next twenty seemed to stretch for double that time and
he gradually relaxed. He looked at his watch. Ten past
midnight. If anything was going to happen, it should
happen soon. He recomposed his limbs and leaned back in
the chair; his eyes pricked and he wished he was in bed.
Already he felt the expedition was a failure.

The coke in the stove crackled and re-adjusted itself with
a rushing noise; in the peace of the kitchen it sounded like
an avalanche. Barnaby sat upright sharply and felt guilty.
He had dozed off: that would not do. He stood up,
conscious of every sound he made, and looked around the
room. Nothing had changed; it looked exactly as it had done
when he had arrived breathless and expectant only—he
looked at his watch again—only two hours before. Yet
something was different. He puzzled briefly, then realized it
was only the moon. Originally it had played on the coarse
grain of the well-scrubbed table; now it had moved to the
floor giving the red tiles a delicacy of shade they never
experienced in the daytime.

He looked out of the window and up at the moon. He
stood on one foot and then the other; and he stared at the
blackness of the trees surrounding the house. He wondered
whether to call the whole thing off. A lick of flame spurted
upward from Gregg's bonfire, ending a period of smoldering; blue and white flames competed for mastery, a funnel

of gray smoke rose above the line of the trees. Barnaby watched, fascinated. Then, suddenly, he understood, and his understanding was tinged with fury.

"My God!" he exclaimed hoarsely. "The bonfire! Why didn't I think of the bonfire?" Poised at the moment of comprehension, he stood motionless. Then he turned and dashed from the room.

The air was cool after the close atmosphere of the kitchen, but he scarcely noticed it as he emerged into the night. His eyes were on the bonfire, thirty yards away, whose flames flickered and danced, throwing grotesque shadows on the surrounding trees. On one side, dark and vague, a bent figure was prodding at the fire with a stick, sending up showers of sparks.

Barnaby edged forward, hoping he was invisble in the shadow of the building, but he had gone only a few yards when a sharp dip in the ground brought him staggering to his knees for the second time that evening. The figure by the fire immediately jerked upright, caught sight of the movement behind him, and fled toward the nearest cover.

Relieved of all need for caution, Barnaby lunged forward and arrived at the bonfire before the unknown had reached the shelter of the trees. Seizing the first thing that came to hand—a clumsy piece of branch—he probed the fire and withdrew what appeared to be the remains of a pair of trousers. The flames died almost at once and vigorous stamping soon reduced the areas still smoldering, but he could not afford to waste time with evidence when he might miss the main chance of catching the criminal himself, so he threw the smoking remnant into the near-by greenhouse and set off in pursuit.

The fugitive had disappeared into the small cluster of trees crowning a low hillock just beyond the bonfire. Once among the trees himself, Barnaby realized they were so sparsely spaced as to give little chance of concealment; accordingly he pushed straight through, assuming that panic would have driven the other to do the same. When he broke cover on the far side of the spinney, he found his reasoning justified. Before him, white in the moonlight, and falling away to thick woods at the bottom of the valley, stretched an open expanse of parkland. At first it seemed deserted, a midnight tableau petrified by the moon. Then, small and insignificant, yet isolated like a fly on the wall, a running figure detached itself from a tree halfway down the slope and headed for the Long Gallow Woods.

Barnaby's response did more credit to his youthful spirit than mature experience. Forcing his way through a low hedge, he covered a ditch with one leap and broke into a gallop as he landed on the grass beyond. His style was ungainly but effective: his long legs, so curiously jointed, seemed to move in slow motion yet consumed the ground in vast strides; his arms flailed wildly. It was easy going at first; he was fresh, the ground sloped gently away from him, and a little action made a change from sitting hunched and despondent in the kitchen. But he had not been running for many seconds before he realized he ought to have enlisted other help before setting out on his midnight vigil. It needed a younger man than he was for this steeple-chasing and with an assistant he would probably have made a capture by now. Nevertheless, he was no mean performer and he was definitely closing the gap.

The figure ahead, still small and indistinct, knew he was gaining. At least twice it checked its headlong flight and the blanched mask of its face flashed over its shoulder. Barnaby knew the frightened, hunted look it must bear and even felt a certain sympathy; but he might have saved the sympathy for himself, for it looked as though his pursuit was to be fruitless. Although he was catching up, his quarry was getting ominously near to the safety of the thick woodland ahead, and as yet he felt no spark of recognition—he could not even tell whether it was a man or a woman, though its speed and apparent stamina suggested the former. They were on the floor of the valley now and the pace was slowing. He no longer had the advantage of the higher ground and slight undulations meant that he could not always keep the figure in sight. Twice he dipped, and twice he found the unknown still ahead; a third time, and when he breasted the rise the park was empty. The woodland which loomed before him had swallowed his prey. He slackened to a trot until he, too, was among the trees; then he dropped to a dejected walk, his thighs weak and limp, his breath coming in painful gasps.

He felt giddy, there was a roaring noise in her ears, and his heart was thumping against his ribs. Apart from these purely physical sensations, he was angry. If he had given the matter a moment's consideration, he would not have come tearing away from the school as he had done; even as he pounded the last exhausting yards into the wood, he saw that he had been lured hopelessly out of position. By cutting back up the drive, or across the park at another point, his quarry could easily get back to the school without being seen, and once inside he could vanish into normality as easily as he had disappeared in the wood. He had been fooled. No, that was too strong—it was hard to believe that he had been led astray deliberately—he had fooled himself, like the greenest constable on the beat. And perhaps hardest of all, his vanity was wounded; apparently he could not run half a mile without coming near to a state of collapse.

The silence of the wood was oppressive. As he recovered, Barnaby listened. A remote chance still remained. It was not improbable that the fugitive had also taken the chance of a rest; and if he had, he would soon be moving; he could not afford to wait too long. Ten minutes passed; but nothing disturbed the sleeping wood except the scufflings of small creatures going about their nocturnal business. Barnaby, his nerves taut, began to feel he had been creeping around among trees for the whole of his life, like a strange symbol of frustration straying from a Bergman film. And he had pins and needles in one foot.

It was no good; he refused to wait any longer. Wryly he wondered what Lord Brisham would think if he knew. "Go straight to the top. Get the best men . . ." Serve him right anyway. Barnaby made his way back to the greenhouse to recover the one thing of value gained from his expedition. The acrid smell of burning greeted him at the door and for a second he thought he had been cheated even of his consolation prize. Certainly the trousers had smoldered on after he had left them and were now barely recognizable. But some of the waistband remained, together with a label of some sort; they would repay inspection in the morning.

Inspector Barnaby walked back to the village much chastened—an unusual experience for him. It seemed particularly unfair that the object of his pursuit was probably in bed before he was.

CHAPTER SIXTEEN

BARNABY did not conceal his chagrin from Graham when they breakfasted early in the low-beamed dining room of the De Mallet Arms. In between the appearances of a pallid waitress, he outlined the depressing story of his night's work and Graham was suitably sympathetic. Secretly he was relieved to find his superior was fallible; the tense concentration of the hunt the previous day had led him to suspect otherwise.

After breakfast the trousers were examined in detail but with disappointing results. They were undoubtedly a man's pair, but were so charred, and so little remained—a small section of waistband, the zip-fly, and a short piece of leg down to one knee—that it was impossible to deduce their size, or even their original color. The label, which was just readable, showed they were mass produced by a well-known Northern firm and might have been bought at any tailor's. With nothing beneath the knee it was likely there would be any traces of chlorine, though the mere fact that someone had tried to destroy them after Barnaby's calculated warning was proof enough. Forensic might get something out of them but Barnaby was not hopeful.

In the meanwhile he decided to check the stories of Gregory and Jordon. He questioned the landlord, a florid man of enormous girth, who had once hoped to turn his pub into a fashionable country club to attract wealthy Bristol suburbanites, had failed, and now drank away the profits he had never made. His name was Rugg.

"Yes, I remember 'em both," he replied. "The new one—Gregory—sat in the lounge bar and looked as miserable as sin. He drank about a couple of pints—in halves," he added with disgust.

"And Jordon?"

"Well, of course, I know him, even though he's only been to the pub once of twice. Everybody knows everybody else here. He's a funny chap. Very learned, so I'm told— history and so on. He gave a lecture in the village once." Rugg's stomach heaved as he drew breath.

"What about the night before last?"

"Very odd," replied Rugg, "very odd indeed. As I said before, he's only been in here once or twice and he's never had more than the odd pint. But that night—"—he whistled through his teeth—"he drank gallons. And he had a row with old Charlie Palmer about Trade Unions. Eventually— and it was still early—I suggested he went home. To be honest I was frightened he'd be sick on the floor. He went like a lamb."

"Can you remember how early it was?"

"About half-past eight. I remember because I'd never seen anybody quite so drunk quite so early." A chuckle of approval rumbled up from his subterranean regions.

"What about Gregory? When did he go?"

"He was so quiet I didn't really notice him. But it must have been about the same time as Jordon. He wasn't there when the village cricket team came in and that was just after half-past."

"Do you think anybody might have seen them outside?"

"Could be," replied Rugg, shrugging. "You could try old Mrs. Thatcher over the road. She sees most things. In the winter she peers out from behind her lace curtains; in the summer she sits out in the street. Some people say she's batty, but she's a shrewd old bird really." He laughed and made an ineffectual attempt to hitch up his trousers.

"Is she likely to be up by this time?" asked Barnaby, glancing at the clock, which showed a quarter to eight.

"Yes," boomed Rugg. "She's up at the crack of dawn. Says that when you're old you can't afford to miss the daylight—you haven't much more to come."

Barnaby crossed the road and knocked on the door of the cottage Rugg had indicated. A dog barked and a flicker of curtain betrayed the internal watcher. After a lengthy delay, the door opened to reveal a small woman, dressed in black, whose wizened face was dominated by a pair of penetrating eyes.

"Yes?" she said discouragingly.

"Excuse me, Mrs. Thatcher, but I'm a police inspector and Mr. Rugg at the—"

"Ah, the murder." She nodded her head with understanding. "Come in, Officer. I thought you might come to see me." Her voice was harsh, but her lined face smiled. She turned and shuffled into the tiny front room, where a mongrel terrier regarded Barnaby with suspicion. "Sit down, Officer."

He sat down, looking around at the hundred-and-one photographs, pictures and ornaments that cluttered the room. Mrs. Thatcher lowered herself carefully into the winged, high-backed chair opposite.

"I knew you'd come," she said. "I knew you'd want to

hear some gossip. There's not much escapes me here, you know. For instance—" She waggled a finger. "For instance," she repeated, "there's Doreen Carpenter and young Wilfred, the vicar's son. I don't think the vicar would approve if he's seen what *I* saw. I may be old, but I get about, you know. And I don't make much noise. Not that they were listening to anything but themselves, and they wouldn't have expected an old busybody like me to be looking into the old tithe barn." She shook her head. "I don't know what the monks would have said."

"Probably went there themselves," thought Barnaby, wondering when he could interrupt without appearing rude. "Now, Mrs. Thatcher," he said brightly, "if I may—"

"Call me Granny," she broke in. "Everybody else does. I'm known as Granny Thatcher in the village."

"Very well—Granny," he said reluctantly. "Now I want to ask you about some people up at the school. To begin with—"

Petulantly she waved his words away. "If only you'd listen," she said, "instead of trying to do all the talking, you might hear something interesting. It's always the same with you town folk. You can't never stop talking. Now like I was saying. The vicar wouldn't approve of the carrying on in the old barn—and no more do I," she added righteously. "But he isn't the only one. The new master up at the school didn't think much to it either—leastways he was watching the hay the other evening just before I got there. Peeping in at the door, he was, and nipped off sharpish when he saw me coming. If you ask me, he's sweet on Doreen Carpenter himself and was keeping an eye on his rival. He hasn't got a chance, mind you—him and his glasses and bird watching. That's no 'obby for a man, you know."

"When was this?" asked Barnaby, realizing that if he wanted any information he would have to play the game according to Granny Thatcher's rules and feeling a prick of interest at the mention of Gregory.

"About a week ago. It's this hot weather—it always plays havoc with the birth rate. Do you know, Officer, one reason why the Puritans cut down the maypoles was—"

Barnaby did not see that maypoles or Gregory's supposed passion for Doreen Carpenter were going to help him, but he took his cue. He interrupted: "I was going to ask you about Mr. Gregory. Did you notice either him or Mr. Jordon coming out of the pub on the night of the murder?"

"Yes, I did. Mr. Jordon came out first. I think he'd had too much and was taking his time. He propped himself up in the doorway for a bit then sat down on that bench over there on the Green." She pointed out of the window over Barnaby's shoulder. "He sat there for about ten minutes with his head in his hands—recovering, I suppose. He was still there when Mr. Gregory came out. Mr. Gregory walked toward him to start with and I thought he was going to speak to him, but he seemed to change his mind at the last moment and turned away down the High Street. Mr. Jordon sat a little while longer, then he went off up the High Street—"

"*Up* the High Street? You mean that Mr. Jordon went in the opposite direction to Mr. Gregory?"

"Oh, yes. Mr. Gregory went back to the lane that leads to the main gates, but Mr. Jordon went up past the church. He could get back into the park that way, you know, across the fields. I expect he didn't want to meet anybody after having so much to drink. He didn't come back this way, that's for certain."

It seemed a fair assumption and it was possible that Jordon's behavior was as innocent as Granny Thatcher suggested, but Barnaby saw that his roundabout route through the village and the park would have taken him perilously close to the swimming bath. What was perhaps more significant was the fact that he had seen fit to omit all mention of this detour from his own account.

Granny Thatcher was talking again, her eyelids drooping as though she was about to fall asleep. "My mother was a parlor-maid up at the Court in the days when the Openshaws were there, you know. And now my grand-daughter Mary works there—I think she was the last person to see Mr. Carter alive."

Barnaby had been about to make his excuses, for he saw Graham waiting with the car outside the De Mallet Arms, but this new connection delayed him.

"Ah, yes, that would be Miss Croft. I haven't met her yet. Do you know if she has any ideas about Mr. Carter's death?"

Granny Thatcher was very close to sleep now; her eyes were glazed and she was moving forward and backwards with a gentle rocking motion.

"I should say she has," she replied. "You'd better ask her yourself, but she's a sharp pair of ears on her and she's not above listening at doors. Ask her what she heard in the Headmaster's study at the beginning of term when. . . . Ask what Miss Grant was . . . Ask. . . ."

Her voice trailed away and she was asleep. Barnaby slipped out of the room, bending low under a couple of murderous beams; the small black figure behind him, still swaying softly, was emitting a soft rhythmical whistling sound.

Within five minutes Barnaby and Graham were once more turning into the now familiar school drive. Arriving at the front door, the inspector gave Graham final instructions before dispatching him to investigate the pubs Maitland claimed to have visited, while he himself strolled on to the terrace and gazed out over the park. In the light of day he could not help feeling that his moonlight chase had been part of a depressing dream and the fugitive a mere figment of his imagination. Somehow in the bright colors of the morning the school, the pavilion, the hedge along which he had crept, had acquired a reality they had lacked in the stark black and white of the night.

"Good morning, Inspector." Warren, begowned and smiling affably, approached from the main door. "Difficult to imagine crime on a morning like this, isn't it?"

"Yes," replied Barnaby shortly. To himself he thought: "And difficult to imagine a terrified murderer flying for his life over this park only few hours ago." Aloud he said: "Prayers at nine, I believe you said, Mr. Warren?"

Even as he spoke, Mark Begbie sauntered out of the central door and began to toll the bell. More swiftly than usual—for Warren's disciplinary grip was already tightening up the slack in the previous administration—the school assembled.

Once again rows of boys faced a row of masters. To Begbie, still feeling the effects of the previous day's experience, it seemed like a grim charade played out for a mocking audience of gods and as he took his appointed place in the line of tubular chairs, he glanced up at the bogus minstrel gallery half expecting to see a row of grinning deities. Instead he saw Barnaby sitting in one corner, his lean face surveying both boys and staff. Begbie looked at his colleagues: Warren, calm and assured, getting up to take prayers; Gregory expressionless and looking half asleep; Jordon sitting with his mouth open, as though the pace of recent events had been too much for him; Maitland smiling confidently.

Prayers were short and soon over, their content having a secular emphasis that would have gone far to satisfy a humanist; Warren did not refer to Carter's death. Afterwards he made a few announcements briskly and ended by saying that Inspector Barnaby of Scotland Yard wanted to say something to the school. An excited buzz immediately broke out only to be quelled by a firm 'That's enough' from Warren.

The inspector had been seen by most of the school during his investigations of the previous day and, with the unerring accuracy of small boys, had already been accorded a nickname—'the galloping hairpin.' Now all heads turned as, coming down from the gallery by a narrow circular stair, the object of much speculation, considerable awe and no little amusement made a theatrical appearance. The gangling figure mounted the dais and turned to face his audience.

"Boys," he said, speaking slowly and with emphasis, "you all know why I am here and what my job is. You probably know that I was busy for most of yesterday. What you don't know is that I am still a long way from the truth about your Headmaster's death." He paused and there was a perceptible shuffle of unease from the masters behind him. "I need all the help from masters and boys that I can get. To be more precise, I want to know whether any of you saw or heard anything suspicious on the night Mr. Carter died, or earlier in the day perhaps, or one of you may have spotted something peculiar earlier in the term. Just think it over and ask yourself if anything happened which you thought was unusual—anything at all. It might be something quite big, it might be something quite small. Whatever it was, I want to know all about it. It may well be the missing link I'm after. Now try and think very hard, and don't be frightened to come and see me. I shall be up in Mr. Carter's study."

"Not bad for a policeman," remarked Maitland, when Barnaby had withdrawn. "He got across."

"Yes, thoroughly competent," agreed Warren. "Crisp and to the point, no waffling. Unlike . . ." He stopped abruptly.

Maitland laughed insensitively. "Unlike our late lamented Headmaster, you mean. I should say so."

Begbie looked at Maitland curiously, as though realizing for the first time that he did not like him.

Upstairs in the study, Barnaby took off his coat and sat down at the desk. The room was bathed in sunlight and it was already very warm. This was the part of a case he liked least, the solid grind of routine sift and search. Somehow it was always neatly shelved in detective stories, or else palmed off on some sergeant, who thereupon vanished from view for at least two chapters while his superior, not deigning to soil his hands with such dull business, made a series of brilliant deductions from the flimsiest evidence or devised some grand stratagem which made all his hard work irrelevant.

He was about to pull open the top drawer when a slip of paper sticking in the corner of the blotter caught his attention. He picked it up, together with a photograph of some sort attached to it by a paperclip. It was plain white writing paper and on it was a brief message, typewritten in capitals:

YES, HE SURVIVED. BUT HE MIGHT AS WELL BE DEAD.

The photograph was a clipping from a newspaper, curling at the edges and yellowing with age; though far from distinct, it appeared to show a heap of rubble surrounded by a number of men wearing dark uniforms and tin hats.

CHAPTER SEVENTEEN

BARNABY puzzled over the photograph and its anonymous message. The implied accusation and the bitter note behind it suggested he might have stumbled on something relevant to Carter's death, but the circumstances of the photograph and their relationship to the message were wholly obscure. The tin hats of the men looking at the rubble reminded him of London during the Blitz, but there was nothing to indicate time or place and it could equally well have been an earthquake disaster in a remote part of the world he had never heard of. As for its significance for Carter, there was no evidence at all. It was not clear whether he had received it—Barnaby could find no envelope—or whether he was going to send it to someone else. Reluctantly, for he felt his find might well be important if only he could put it into context, he returned to his search of the desk.

Most of the papers were letters about the boys: mothers fussing over their health or clothes; fathers inquiring into lack of academic progress—or, occasionally, explaining failure to pay termly bills; Public Schools asking for confidential reports on prospective entrants; letters from Old

Boys who proudly announced the birth of a son and asked to put his name down for a place some seven years hence. Carter's private correspondence seemed to be small: a few letters from the sister in Ireland, and batches of receipts for bills which had all been promptly paid. From the written evidence, his private life appeared devoid of emotion: he had neither friends nor enemies.

The last three drawers yielded copious historical notes and letters relating to Carter's research. Barnaby glanced through them briefly and was about to dismiss them when he noticed the most recent letter, from Cutts and Pennington, the publishers, who professed themselves delighted to accept Carter's manuscript on the Levellers. He would not have attached any importance to this letter had he not noticed that it was dated on the previous Tuesday, which meant that Carter had received it on the day he died. He could see no obvious relevance, but it was the type of detail he never overlooked. The notes themselves, and a pile of photostats of seventeenth-century pamphlets heavily annotated in Carter's hand, looked dull in the extreme. He thumbed them through, wondering that a man could spend his spare time on such tedious material. The rest of the study produced nothing of interest whatsoever. A metal filing cabinet which promised much contained nothing but records of school finances and papers dealing with an appeal recently launched for a science laboratory and new library—a dual aim designed, as a covering letter from the organizer shrewdly observed, to appeal to both sides of the cultural fence. There were two more batches of notes: one on the *Historia Brittonum* of Nennius, the other on the origins of the Wansdyke.

Barnaby returned to Carter's bedroom, which led off the study. Here there was little to hold his attention at first. There were plenty of books, mostly history and fiction, some evangelical pamphlets, and a number of circulars from the Ministry of Education notable only for their depressing use of the English language; but otherwise the room was barren and Barnaby had almost given up hope of finding anything useful when he came upon a locked suitcase under a jumble of clothes at the bottom of the wardrobe. He opened it with a little brute force and turned the contents on to the bed.

Before him on the bedspread was a pile of photographs like the one he had found on the desk. They had been taken from different newspapers and the angle of the picture varied, but each showed a pile of rubble and onlookers in uniform. However, this time there was more information. Some of the photographs had captions—*A London rescue* and, more graphically, *A man came out of this alive*—and other cuttings told the story in detail. A block of flats in Kensington had received a direct hit during a German night raid in 1941; four people had been killed and another ten had been pulled from the debris. The rescue operations had been halted and it was assumed there were no more casualties. Two days later a child playing near the ruins had been frightened by noises. The police were called and when digging was resumed another man was pulled out alive. He had been taken to hospital, where it was hoped he would recover from his ordeal. Attached to each cutting was a piece of paper with the terse comment he already knew: YES, HE SURVIVED. BUT HE MIGHT AS WELL BE DEAD.

Even now, with the additional information, Barnaby could make little sense of his discovery. It looked as though someone had sent the cuttings to Carter and the repeated message suggested they had arrived over a period of time, otherwise one message would have covered the lot. But there were no envelopes to show when they had come or where they had originated. He turned the pieces of paper

over again, trying to recognize each newspaper by the
journalistic style. Then he realized he was looking at
something he had missed before. Instead of a straight-
forward account of the incident, it was a comment taken
from a short editorial:

One Man's Life

*In time of war the currency of life depreciates. When
death is all around, one death more or less does not seem
to matter much. We are reminded of this frightening and
inevitable truth by the incident earlier this week in which
a man was left to die amidst the ruins of his home. It is
perhaps churlish to criticize the rescue team, for they
saved ten lives and left the scene to cope with another
bombed building. But the fact remains that they left for a
second task before they had finished the first and
insufficient care was taken to find out whether there were
any more survivors. In this instance all was well: the man
was found, though not before he had undergone a
harrowing experience. Another time he might not be so
lucky. It is to be hoped that in future rescue squad leaders
will ensure, so far as they are able, that there are no
more victims left in one disaster before they move on to
another.*

Barnaby grunted at the characteristically smug editorial
tone, but it clarified the picture and suggested two possibilities. Either Carter had been the man entombed and
someone with a singularly unpleasant turn of mind wished
he had stayed there; or, and this seemed the more likely,
Carter had been involved in some way with the rescue
operations and was being blamed for the sufferings of the
man left in the rubble. Assuming the latter, the next step was
to consider who might be bearing the grudge and carrying

out a campaign of planned persecution. Warren was old
enough to have been the victim, but Barnaby had heard of
his army career and it was unlikely, though not impossible,
that he had been in Kensington in 1941; moreover, there was
no hint of the man being a soldier and that would have
surely merited comment in wartime. But age was only a
limiting factor in one sense. Any of the other members of
the staff, male or female, could be relations of the rescued
man—sons, daughters, wives, the possible permutations
were endless. Nevertheless, it was with a feeling of relief
that he put the cuttings back in the suitcase and took it into
the study. Up till now the only visible motive had been the
general dislike of Carter's methods, a possibility but not one
he was inclined to favor. Now he had something more
tangible, so he rang the Yard and asked for research into the
Blitz incident. In particular, he wanted the personal and
family background of the buried man and, if possible, his
subsequent history.

Carter's drawing-room revealed nothing new. More notes
on the Levellers, this time centerd on the personalities of
Lilburne, Walwyn and Overton, and several letters from
archivists, but nothing of interest to Barnaby. He returned to
the study, where the telephone was ringing.

The call brought the result of the post mortem, which was
exactly as expected. Carter had died from the stab wound
and death had been virtually instantaneous. That tidied
away one loose end. It also gave him the spur he needed to
postpone further search of Carter's academic work. He was
becoming very bored with the fanatical Levellers and the
illegible writing of Carter's intellectual correspondents.
This reminder that a man had been brutally murdered
brought him back to the present. In any case, he suspected
he had already found anything likely to be important.

Before he could decide on his next move, however, there

was a knock at the door. In response to his second invitation, a boy with prominent ears came into the room. He hesitated a moment, adjusted a heavy pair of spectacles, then advanced confidently.

"Excuse me, sir," he said with aplomb. "I think I can help you."

"Good. Come and sit down. What's your name?"

"Bennet, sir."

"Right-ho, Bennet—Now, what do you think I ought to know?" Barnaby was trying to temper his normal brusque approach with a certain bluff cheeriness.

"I sleep in the Classical dormitory, sir—it's full of dreary Greek gods—and it overlooks the front of the school. Well, I couldn't sleep, sir, so I got up and looked out of the window. That was when I saw him, sir."

"Him?"

"Yes, sir. It was definitely a man. He was creeping about as though he didn't want anybody to see him, and when he wasn't under the cover of the trees he ran. He looked very suspicious, sir." He was obviously pleased with the words. He repeated them: "Very suspicious."

Barnaby nodded his approval. "You have been very observant, Bennet. Now tell me—"—the inspector leaned forward confidentially and lowered his voice—"When did you see this person?"

"Last night, sir. I don't know what time it was because my watch is bust, but it must have been very late. I think the moon woke me up."

"*Last* night," said Barnaby incredulously.

"Oh yes, sir. He was tall and thin, and sort of bendy. I saw him hiding down by the cricket pavilion, then he ran off to the end of the school. He had an enormous shadow."

"I see. Well, that's most helpful." Barnaby smiled bleakly. He was having difficulty in relishing the full flavor of the joke; it did not look as though his night's prowl had been any more successful at the beginning that it had been at the end.

He was about to shoo Bennet back to his form when the boy produced a pale blue envelope. "Oh, by the way, sir, Mr. Jordon asked me to give you this. I almost forgot."

Barnaby shepherded the boy out of the room, giving strict instructions that he should tell no one what he had seen. As the door closed he opened the envelope.

The note inside was short and in a spidery hand that accorded well with its writer's appearance:

Inspector:
  I should like to speak to you privately. I shall be in the old railway cutting at 12:15 p.m.

                                        D. Jordon.

CHAPTER EIGHTEEN

THE previous morning the school had been stunned by the news of Carter's death; now the reaction had set in and everywhere there was an air of tense expectancy. Jordon was having a particularly trying morning. The moment he joined IIb for the last period before break the chatter faded away; every face looked at him curiously. He affected not to notice the atmosphere as he organized his books on the desk. Out of the corner of one eye he saw a hand rise.

"Yes, Gordon?"

"I hope you don't mind me asking, sir, but could you tell us what is going on?"

"I beg your pardon?" When he did not know how to answer, Jordon always played for time.

"Can you put us in the picture, sir? Who are the police going to arrest?"

Now it was Jordon's turn again. He was tempted to make some withering remark about 'idle speculation,' realized it would not be understood, so said weakly, "I don't know. Now let us do some history. Where . . . ?"

He was not going to get off so lightly. "Have they interviewed you, sir?"

"We are not concerned with the police inquiry, Gordon. Let them get on with their job and we will get on with ours." Fatally he added: "Yes, as a matter of fact they have."

"Did they believe your story, sir?"

Jordon removed his spectacles with an air of resignation. He eyed the boy wearily but without malice. "I have no intention of continuing this charade, Gordon. Open your notebooks at the diagram of Morton's Fork."

The display of firmness was too late; the hounds could not be called off. "I'll bet it was done with that knife you confiscated from Manton, sir," said another boy.

Jordon went ashen. "You are quite right, Leggatt. It was. It was Manton's knife all right. Now open your notebook or I shall strike you."

Maitland had no intention of teaching in such unsettled conditions. He set his form more written work, put a senior boy in charge, and set off to find Linda Grant. She was in her room looking miserable.

"What have you done with your boys?" she asked.

"Set the little beasts an essay which I shan't bother to mark. They're all hysterical with excitement this morning— I don't suppose you can blame them. You should hear the chaos in Jordon's room."

"I'm worried, Peter."

"Nothing to fret about, darling. The bean pole isn't interested in us. Give us a kiss."

"No, not now." She pulled away irritably and moved to the window.

"All right," he said indifferently. "What did you tell Barnaby last night?"

"What you told me to. But I didn't like his eyes. I'm sure he didn't believe me."

"Nonsense. That's his professional expression. He's paid to be sceptical."

"Did anybody see us, do you think?"

"No, of course not. Who could have done?"

"I don't know, but I had an odd feeling we were being watched."

Maitland laughed coarsely. "That was just your puritanical conscience. You get it from your Grandmama."

"What about Dennis?"

"Tight as a lord. It was all he could do to find the path home. Anyway, I expect he was wondering what dear Alice would say. It's probably the first time he's rolled up drunk in all their married life. Now you, my dear, will have to get used to it." Again he laughed and made to put on arm around her.

She moved away coldly. "I'm not sure we're going to marry, Peter. Not with this hanging over us."

"What do you mean?"

"Doesn't it matter to you who killed Carter?"

"Not particularly. And don't pretend you've lost any sleep over it either. Without putting too fine an edge on it, it's fallen very conveniently for us, hasn't it?"

"Yes, very conveniently—that's just what I mean."

The staff room was quiet at break. It was usually a sociable gathering but today a pall of gloom had settled.

"The tea's cold and the biscuits are damp," said Begbie at length. "I wonder how they manage it in the middle of a heatwave."

"We're on the front page now." Warren spoke from behind his newspaper without looking up. " 'The Claydon

Prior Mystery'—not very original. I've been fending off the Press all the morning."

No one took this up. The sun streamed in through the windows, revealing how long it was since anyone had cleaned them.

Begbie spoke again: "Well, who's got an alibi?"

Everyone looked up, but there was no reply.

"No one?"

"Do you think we should talk about it?" This from Gregory.

"Yes, I do." Warren put his cup down carefully by his chair. "I agree with you, Mark. It's no good bottling it all up inside—and I for one have yet to be convinced that we have a murderer at Claydon."

They were all watching Warren now.

"You see," he went on, "I imagine we're all too frightened to say anything in case it looks as though we're guilty. And on top of that we're looking over our shoulders to see if the man sitting next to us, whom we've always treated as a colleague, is really a cold-blooded killer. But the school must go on, so it would be as well if we treated each other as normal human beings again."

"I've got an alibi of sorts." Maitland laid down his paper with a flourish and smiled around the room. "I was out on a pub-crawl. I'd had Crawford in to go through one of his Common Entrance papers after tea and that was enough to drive anyone to drink. I gave the sleuth a list of the pubs I went to. When I got back—about eleven-thirty—I didn't see anyone, though I think I heard John and Mark talking in Mark's room. I retired to my virtuous couch just as soon as I could get my clothes off, and yesterday morning I heard the news at the same time as everyone else."

Maitland sat back and lit a cigarette. Gregory, smiling oddly, traced a careful pattern on his paper with a red Biro.

Jordon shifted in his seat and adjusted his spectacles; he seemed about to speak.

But Begbie spoke next. "Not much to tell," he said apologetically. "I had my supper and listened to the Krovsky concert. *Leonora No. 3* and the Brahms B flat Piano Concerto, then the *Water Music* as a 'fill-in' after that foolhardy Hungarian girl collapsed—the wretched Harty arrangement, of course. Why they don't stick to the original version I can't imagine." He waved his hand toward Warren. "After that you came in, at the beginning of that talk on place names. Remember all that stuff about Woden, Tig and so on?"

"The trouble is," broke in Maitland, "that we don't know exactly when Carter was killed. Did Barnaby tell anyone?"

He looked hopefully around, and got a shock. For standing in the open doorway was Barnaby himself.

"No, I didn't mention it, Mr. Maitland," he said, "for obvious reasons. I'm glad, gentlemen, that you are sticking to your stories. I apologize for coming in uninvited, but the door was open." He did not sound apologetic at all.

Warren pulled a chair forward. "Please sit down, Inspector. The tea is cold, I'm afraid."

"No thank you, Mr. Warren, I must be getting along. No doubt I shall be seeing one or two of you later."

With which enigmatic remark he closed the door.

"So much for clearing the air," said Begbie. "I feel worse than before."

CHAPTER NINETEEN

WHEN Barnaby left the staff room, he went outside and made for the front drive; reluctantly, for the prospect did not excite him, he had decided to see Mrs. Jordon before keeping his clandestine appointment with her husband.

The Lodge was a sad building standing in a clump of trees at the main entrance. Its dull red brick merged darkly with the surrounding greenery and although the sun scorched down on the drive and melted the tar, only the faintest rays filtered through to the Lodge. Barnaby relished the coolness as he turned under the trees.

Alice Jordon asked him into the kitchen, where she was preparing lunch. To his surprise and relief he could barely recognize her as the same woman who had caused the commotion of the previous evening. Her yellow hair still stood out challengingly and the lines on her face were taut, but all the life had gone out of her eyes and voice. From an hysterical woman exuding nervous energy, she had become a drab and faded replica of her husband. She did not seem surprised to see him and made no reference to their first meeting. As for the night of the murder, she was unable to recall anything with precision.

"Did your husband get back before or after nine o'clock?" pressed Barnaby.

"I really couldn't say, Inspector."

"Perhaps it will come back better if you try to remember how you spent the evening. Were you at home all the time yourself?"

"No—I didn't get in till after seven. I'd been shopping late in Wells and had to wait for the bus."

"What did you do when you first arrived home?"

"I don't remember—Oh, yes—I did some ironing, then I had some supper. After that I settled down with the wireless and some mending."

"What did you listen to?"

"Oh, nothing in particular. There was a concert of some sort and I just had it on in the background. I didn't listen properly—I'm not very interested in classical music."

Barnaby was beginning to wonder if she was interested in anything at all. "Didn't a pianist collapse?" he prompted.

She seemed to hesitate, but it might have been his imagination.

"Yes—you're right. The woman playing the concerto fainted. I remember it now. I didn't pay much attention at the time."

"But had your husband returned by then?"

At last he had circled back to his original question. This was hard work.

"No—he hadn't." She stirred something in a saucepan.

"Was it long afterward?"

At length it came to light that Jordon had returned at around nine-thirty, when she had been watching a play on television. She knew he'd had too much to drink and he'd gone straight to bed.

"Is your husband happy at the school?"

She waved her hand ineffectively. "He's never been happy teaching. He can't keep order and he hasn't much in common with little boys. Somehow he can't get down to their level or bring them up to his. And small boys can be very cruel, you know. No, he doesn't enjoy teaching," she concluded.

Barnaby was encouraged by this sudden burst of information. "Why does he teach, then?"

"Why does anyone? It provides a home, I suppose." She shrugged and looked hopelessly around the little kitchen with the condensation clinging to the walls.

"Last night, Mrs. Jordon, you made an uncomplimentary remark about Mr. Maitland. Was it justified?"

"Certainly."

"Would you care to say any more about it—in confidence, of course?"

"No—I was unwise to say what I did."

"Perhaps. To come back to your husband. Does he often drink?"

"No."

"Have you any idea why he did yesterday?"

"No, none at all."

"Have you any theory about Mr. Carter's death, Mrs. Jordon?"

Her answer was expressionless and utterly predictable. "No," she said.

Before leaving, Barnaby asked to see over the house. Only Jordon's study, filled with books and comfortable in an untidy way, relieved the overall impression of dreariness. He glanced around quickly but saw nothing to interest him except the typewriter on the desk. He picked up a piece of paper and typed the message he had found earlier: YES, HE SURVIVED. BUT HE MIGHT AS WELL BE DEAD. Then he tore it off, folded it, and put it in his pocket for a later comparison. He screwed up the remaining paper and tossed it into the waste-basket. As he did so, it occurred to him that Jordon had been having a clear-out recently. The basket was full and several piles of papers, each held together by a rubber band, lay beside it, also presumably for disposal. Curiously, he stooped and pulled out one of the top sheets.

It was a page of typescript with a heading underlined in red: *John Lilburne: Shades of the Prison House*. Momentarily he could not think where he had heard of Lilburne before, then he remembered that the name had cropped up regularly in the notes he had read only a short while earlier in Carter's study. He thumbed through the other papers and found several more with a familiar ring—*The Putney Debates*, *Mutiny at Ware*, *Executions at Burford*. One was headed *Killing No Murder*, a grim title he recalled seeing in Carter's collection of photostats of seventeenth-century pamphlets. Here was a conncection he had not anticipated and certainly one he did not understand. He made a careful selection and then joined Mrs. Jordon in the kitchen, where she had returned to continue her preparations for lunch.

He said: "I'd like to borrow these for a while. I'll tell your husband I've got them."

"Yes, if you want to. Dennis won't mind." It was the first time she had referred to her husband by his Christian name and she did so with total indifference.

Released from the depressing atmosphere of the Lodge, Barnaby turned off the drive toward the Long Gallow Woods. The mid-day sun was hot, the hum of insects inviting, and he had a good twenty minutes in hand before his meeting with Jordon. Besides, it was time for reflection. He felt for his pipe, scraped out the unsavory remains of his last smoke, refilled it, and used half a dozen matches to get it going properly.

The link between Carter and Jordon was puzzling. As he strolled through the long grass, he took out the pages of typescript and read them over again. At first he thought the two men had been collaborating on some historical project and that Jordon was throwing away his material in despair because Carter's death meant the end of the scheme. But the more he looked at Jordon's papers, the more it seemed they duplicated what he had seen in Carter's study. Then he saw another possibility. Suppose both Carter and Jordon had been researching separately on the same subject unbeknown to each other; and suppose Carter had finished first and had his work accepted for publication. An amazing coincidence, certainly, but he had known stranger ones: it would fit with the publisher's letter and Jordon's odd behavior. And if he was right there was a motive for murder.

Quite suddenly, and in spite of his sympathy for the man, Jordon was emerging as a suspect. His nervous, agitated manner, hitherto disarming, now helped to complete a very different picture. He imagined the introspective Jordon toiling for years on his pet historical patch. Taunted by boys he pitied and could not understand, mocked by colleagues of lesser intellect, and harnessed to an indifferent and insensitive wife, he turned silently to his research, a haven of sanity in a moronic world. Then just when he had his magnum opus on the stocks, the proof he was not the dithering incompetent everyone took him for, he discovered somebody else had cut the ground from under his feet. Barnaby saw that the shock might well be unbearable. Not only was all his work wasted—that was perhaps the least important point—but his dreams of academic distinction were annihilated. For a man whose nervous resources were already nearly exhausted such a discovery might well have catastrophic effects.

A spur of elms crossed his path and caused him to alter

course. He moved into the thicker grass, glancing down at his feet as he lifted them over the tussocks. Then he looked up as he rounded the angle of the trees and stopped in his tracks. Ahead of him, only twenty yards away in a shallow depression fringed by a crescent of trees, a figure was crawling on its hands and knees.

Momentarily, he stood still, taken aback by this odd spectacle. When he saw who it was, he moved forward swiftly.

"Good morning, Mr. Gregory."

The crawling figure froze into immobility. Then Gregory, for he it was, sprang to his feet, brushing the hair from his eyes. His unhealthy face was red, his expression as guilty as Barnaby could have desired. He said: "Good morning, Inspector."

Barnaby said nothing; the expression on his face posed his question.

"I—I expect you wonder what I'm doing. I must look a bit strange."

"I'm sure you know exactly what you're doing, Mr. Gregory."

"Yes, well, as a matter of fact"—he looked sheepish now—"I'm looking for a nest. A lark—it's up there." He pointed over Barnaby's shoulder. A cascade of larksong came from a small dot barely visible over the center of the park. "They build on the ground, you know. I'm sure it's just here somewhere." He indicated the area of crushed grass where he had been kneeling.

Barnaby was tempted to believe him. His original air of guilt had given way to embarrassment.

"Yes," he said, with growing confidence, "I first saw it come down here on the night of Mr. Carter's death."

"On the way back from the pub?"

"That's right."

"You saw it from the drive? It came down just here?" Barnaby looked back through the trees. "Remarkable eyesight, Mr. Gregory. Are you sure you didn't leave the drive? You didn't mention it before."

Gregory was reddening again. "Yes, I think I did. I saw the bird with the glasses and came into the park. It wasn't important—it was only a bird." He hurried on: "I must go now, Inspector. I've got a period in ten minutes and there are some books I must collect from my room."

With as much dignity as he could muster, Gregory set off for the school. Hands in pockets, shoulders slouched, he was not an impressive figure.

Barnaby watched Gregory disappear over the slight eminence that hid the main school building from view, then turned back to the piece of ground that had interested him so much. The patch he had been searching, a small area of beaten grass, stood out clearly. He had obviously been there some time and had confined himself to a strictly limited area. Reluctantly, with the sun hot on his back, Barnaby lowered himself to his knees. He felt faintly ridiculous and was glad he could not be seen from the school.

For five minutes he hunted conscientiously, his fingers exploring the parched, coarse grass. He found nothing. Then he saw something he had not noticed before. Straight ahead of him, about twenty-five yards away in a slight hollow, was another patch of flattened grass. It looked as though Gregory had been searching longer than he had imagined and had concentrated on two distinct spots. Barnaby stood up, stretched himself, and was about to move over to this new discovery when his eye was caught by an object reflecting the light in the grass just beyond the beaten area he was in. He stooped and picked it up. It was a small plastic knob with a milled edge.

The sun streamed relentlessly down, glinting on the piece

of black plastic held between Barnaby's thumb and fore-finger. And looking at the patches of crushed grass again, Barnaby became aware of something else. They were not new: Gregory had been there before.

The larks, its song complete, dropped soundlessly into a field beyond the boundary of the park.

CHAPTER TWENTY

IN THE halcyon days of the Great Western Railway, Claydon Prior had been a junction, with a single-track branch line running to Monk's Bly and Shepton Mallet; but there can have been few lines as blatantly uneconomic as this one and it was among the first to fall when the nationalised railway took a realistic look at its routes after the war. Now, with the track removed, it was just a fading scar twisting through the Mendips, punctuated at intervals by the remains of bridges, stations, and other more permanent manifestations of the railway age. Climbing out of Claydon Prior, the line skirted the school estate in a deep cutting, then swung away northwards, crossing the main track from London on a five-arched viaduct before burrowing into the Claydon Hill tunnel. It was in the cutting, overgrown with ferns and bushes and silent save for the birds who had found it a nesting sanctuary, that Jordon had proposed his meeting with the inspector.

There was no easy path from the school. When the railway ran, it had been counted a virtue that the belt of trees in that part of the park was notably thick and trackless, for it helped to insulate the boys from the hazards of the line. But now Barnaby cursed noisily as he forced his way through the undergrowth, trying to follow the directions obscurely given him by Gregg. At length he emerged from the trees, scaled the boundary wall, and found himself looking directly down the gorse-covered side of the cutting. Jordon was not immediately apparent; then Barnaby smelled tobacco and spotted him sitting halfway down the slope about thirty yards away.

"Careful with your cigarette, Mr. Jordon. This grass is dry."

Jordon, who had not been aware of Barnaby's arrival, stood up. He said, "I know," and adjusted his absurd spectacles.

Barnaby eased himself down the slope and joined him in the shade of a recently rooted sycamore clinging to the side of the cutting. "Now, Mr. Jordon," he said. "What's up?"

"You must forgive me, Inspector, for this melodramatic assignation. The truth is"—he spoke quietly and ran a nervous hand through his hair—"I'm frightened."

Barnaby believed him; he looked frightened.

"You see, I know too much and I don't understand what I know. That's not very clear, I think, so I'll start by admitting that I've been less than honest with you." He looked over the top of his spectacles, which had slipped again.

"The Levellers?" hazarded Barnaby.

"So you know about that, too. I didn't really try to hide it, you know. I just didn't mention it, that's all."

"Sophistry, Mr. Jordon. Tell me about it now."

"There's not much to tell. I've been working on the Levellers for five years and I'm just about ready to publish. Nothing startling, you understand, merely a small monograph. But Carter got there first. I had the material but had barely started writing. Carter had had his script accepted.

He told me so that afternoon . . . down at the swimming bath."

"Yours might have been better."

"Perhaps, but I doubt it." His shoulders had slumped forward and he stared at the far side of the cutting. "It's a narrow field and he told me enough to show he knew his stuff. There wasn't room for both of us—mine was finished."

The double note of a diesel on the main line drifted up from the valley.

"That's not what you brought me down here for, is it?"

"No—no, it was more important." The hunted look returned. "At least I think it's more important now. You see, when I came back from the pub that night, I didn't go straight back to the Lodge. I came back into the park by a small entrance we call Gilley's Gate—it's the gate used by the farmer who grazes his animals on the estate. I was drunk, I felt ill, and I didn't want to go home."

Barnaby looked at him sympathetically, but his senses were alert for any hint of fresh evasion.

"The path from Gilley's Gate comes in from the southern side of the park—you must have crossed it to get here—and it runs around the rear of the swimming bath to the barns and so on behind the main school building. I came up the path some way, then a little short of the pool I left it and went into the trees. I wanted to be sick. It was disgusting."

He looked away down the cutting toward the viaduct and the dark entrance to Claydon Hill tunnel just visible at the far end. "Disgusting," he repeated flatly. He went on: "I cleaned myself up and got back on the track—it's more of a cart-track really, dusty in summer and muddy in winter. But I'd just got there when I heard someone coming. It was Maitland. He didn't see me to begin with and I tried to slip back into the trees—you can imagine that I didn't want to talk to him—but he glanced up at the critical moment and there's no doubt that he spotted me. The strange thing was that he stopped straight away and behaved as though he hadn't seen me at all. I may be wrong, but I had the impression he was waiting for somebody."

"Exactly where was this?"

"About fifty yards this side of the pool. It—it could have been a little more than that, I suppose."

The clarity of Jordon's narrative deserted him when the questions started. Barnaby, standing slightly higher on the slope, loomed over him.

"And the time?"

"I can't be sure. It might have been half-past eight, it could have been nine o'clock. It was getting dark, you know, particularly under the trees. N-no, I couldn't commit myself to a time."

"Would Gregg have seen either of you? He was on the front pitch."

"No. The track is covered by trees or bushes right the way around to the back of the school. I didn't see him."

"Then what did you do?"

"I went home. Not by the shortest route across the open park but through the Long Gallow Woods. I didn't want to meet anyone else."

Barnaby bent forward. "But none of this explains why you are frightened, Mr. Jordon. Maitland probably had as good a reason for being there as you had."

"I know that. And I'm probably being very foolish, Inspector. But he didn't mention being there when we discussed it in the staff room this morning. My impression was that he avoided looking at me altogether."

"But that was in break. You sent me your note before that."

Jordon carefully squeezed the stub of his cigarette and put

it in his pocket. The sun reflected on his glasses and a bead of sweat detached itself and ran down into an eyebrow.

"Yes," he said quietly. "There's more to it. It's irrational, Inspector—I'm sure you don't deal in intuition—but all the same, when I saw Maitland on the path I sensed we were both being watched by someone else. No more than a feeling, you understand, but very strong. And after I'd gone back into the wood I'm certain I heard Maitland's voice. I don't want to get him into trouble, but I must tell the truth now and my impression was that it was all somehow conspiratorial. I'm convinced he met someone. And *they* know I was there. *They* know I . . ." His voice, which had risen, died away suddenly. "That's why I'm frightened."

Barnaby smiled reassuringly. "I don't think you need worry, Mr. Jordon. You've done the right thing to tell me at last, and I'm bound to say that your information is probably as important as you think it is. But"—he spread a hand expansively—"you can stop worrying about your own safety, you know. Whoever killed Carter will lie low now and hope his luck holds. One murder's usually enough, even for a murderer."

Sadly, events were very soon to show how wrong he was.

CHAPTER TWENTY-ONE

LUNCH had been laid out in the study. Graham was already there, halfway through a dry-looking piece of fish. He got up as Barnaby came in.

"I'm afraid I started, sir. No one seemed to know where you were. I hope you don't mind."

"Of course not. Tuck in, Sergeant." He looked more closely at Graham's plate. "I don't think I shall be having much. That bit of fish reminds me of my own schooldays. I recognize that rough, leathery texture."

Graham, who had previously been enjoying his meal uncritically, prodded the fish with suspicion. He said: "Maitland was lying, sir. Nobody remembered seeing him in any of the pubs he mentioned. In fact, sir, Mr. Perkins—he's the landlord of the Barley Mow at Shepton—said it was the first night he hadn't been in for some time. Noticed him by his absence as it were."

"Anyone see his car?"

"No, not a trace of him. He's well known out there, but he certainly wasn't in his usual haunts on Wednesday. I'm not surprised, sir, are you? I thought he was too smart by half."

"I wasn't impressed with him. But it was stupid of him to tell a story that could be checked so easily." Barnaby opened the vegetable dish and peered at the lifeless cabbage. "They don't seem to have changed the vegetables since my day either. I suppose you were spared the rigors of a prep. school, Sergeant?"

"Yes, sir."

"Lucky man. They're hell on earth. They're run on a shoe-string, the food is appalling, and they're always in the most godforsaken parts of the country so nobody can find out. What do you think of Gregory?"

Graham struggled to adjust himself to the rapid turns of the conversation. "Quiet," he replied, "but I think there's more to him than meets the eye."

"I caught him poking about in the woods just now. He's keeping something back and it's my belief he went down there last night when we saw him going across the fields. I found this." He held up the black knob. "Any ideas?"

"Wireless or gramophone tuner I should think, sir. Nothing very remarkable about it."

"That's what I thought. Of course, it may not be connected with this business at all, but it was lying just about where Gregory was searching. I may be wrong, but I suspect he was anxious to find it before we did."

He put the knob away carefully. "I've had an informative talk with Jordon, too. He's admitted he wasn't far from the pool at the critical time and he's got a motive of sorts. Apparently Carter had just had a book accepted for publication on the same subject he'd been working on for five years. His work was useless."

"Would that be strong enough?"

"I've known weaker. Though my impression is that he's

so upset one way and another he's more likely to commit suicide than murder."

"But none of this lot looks like a murderer, sir. Warren, Begbie, Mrs. Quail—they just don't fit."

"And Carter didn't look like a corpse, but that didn't stop somebody making him one." Barnaby became didactic. "You're making the mistake, Graham, of imagining a murderer is a type—like a window-cleaner or a miner. In my experience it's not so. With a few exceptions your killer is a perfectly ordinary citizen, the sort you rub shoulders with every day in the bus. He becomes a murderer when something inside him snaps, when the trappings of generations of civilization drop away and the basic animal takes over. But he doesn't *look* any different; he's still the same person outwardly, but a vital part of him has reverted to the law of the jungle. Once you understand this, then anyone can commit murder—even Jordon."

Graham listened attentively, at the same time clearing a plate of prunes and custard. Barnaby picked at biscuits and cheese.

"I'll bet the boys don't get biscuits and cheese," he grunted. "We never did."

"Did you find anything else, sir?"

"Yes, though it may not be anything to do with us. Someone with a nasty turn of mind was sending Carter anonymous letters. It's a vague story—the Yard's chasing it up."

"Rum sort of place, isn't it?" said Graham reflectively. "Who'd have thought there would be so much to dig up in a little school like this?"

Barnaby did not respond at once; he was gazing out of the window. The boys' lunch was over and they were making the most of free time before afternoon school. An impromptu game of cricket had started. A large boy batted, a large boy bowled, and all the smaller boys fielded. It was not only the food that had not changed.

"No," he replied at last, "it's not really so surprising. When you come to think of it, most of us have a thing or two to keep quiet and I don't suppose the staff of a small prep. school is very different. Besides, the smaller the community, the more there is to hide; everybody wants to know your business."

The bell clanged noisily in front of the school. The cricketers drew stumps and dashed for the front door. Barnaby stood up abruptly.

"Right, Sergeant, this afternoon I want you to see the Croft girl. Old Mrs. Thatcher dropped hints about her eavesdropping outside Carter's study at the beginning of term—something to do with Miss Grant. Find out what it was. And while we're dealing with the Grant angle, you'd better pay a visit to her friend Christine Bradby. Remember, she was up here on Wednesday evening. See if she noticed anything."

Graham set off on his mission and Barnaby was trying to decide what he should do next when the telephone rang. It was the Yard, who had some information on the Kensington Blitz story.

The basic outline was exactly as he had reconstructed it from the cuttings; certain additions clarified the picture. Apparently the buried man had been called Lake. He had recovered from his ordeal physically, but the mental strain had been too much and he was now an incurable inmate of an asylum in Berkshire. "He might as well be dead," murmured Barnaby.

Then came the interest. The man in charge of the rescue squad had been called Carter—Henry Carter. He had been exonerated from all blame after the incident, but had voluntarily retired from the A.R.P. rescue squads soon afterward. So that was it. "Poor devil," Barnaby reflected. "Even his little bit of war effort went wrong."

Sympathy for the dead man was one thing; finding his murderer was another. How did this affect the case? Who might have been prepared to badger Carter with newspaper cuttings, or even murder him, on behalf of an unfortunate lunatic?

The Yard could give only limited help. Lake had been married, with two sons born in 1938 and 1940; there was no trace of either wife or children now. He had last been visited by his wife in 1946; since then there had been no contact between him and his family.

This was weak, but it did something to justify speculation. Assuming the murderer was on the staff—and he made that assumption now without a qualm—few qualified as members of Lake's immediate family from an age point of view. Mrs. Quail was a possibility for the wife, but Maitland and Jordon were the only ones near the right age for the sons, and even they looked too old. Was it conceivable that all three fitted? Hardly; he could not see Jordon as Maitland's brother or, for that matter, Mrs. Quail as the mother of either of them. Of course Warren might be Lake's brother, if he had one, and any of them could be more distant relations. But at the back of his mind was the disturbing thought that the whole Lake business might be a glorious red herring with no relevance to the case whatsoever. After all, he had no proof that the anonymous cuttings originated within the school. The fact that he had found no envelopes proved nothing; Carter might have destroyed them for some reason known only to himself.

While talking to the Yard, Barnaby had decided on his next step. Accordingly, he made his way to the second floor where the resident masters had their rooms. It was time to look at the suspects more closely.

The first door had Gregory's name on it but there was no response when he knocked, so he went in. Gregory was obviously teaching. The room, like its occupant, was dull and lifeless. The desk, the uncomfortable-looking chairs, the small modern bookcase—all were arranged primly. Dead in the center of the window-ledge was a forlorn cactus; equally centrally placed on a small mahogany table stood a wireless. A stuffed hawk of some kind, somewhat lacking in feathers, dominated one corner; prints of birds on the walls and field-glasses hanging behind the door reflected the owner's only hobby. The bedroom, which led off the study, was equally drab and Barnaby found nothing to interest him in either place.

Begbie's room was a marked contrast. A litter of books, magazines and papers covered every article of furniture and overflowed on to the floor; unwashed coffee cups were piled high on the bookcase and a bottle of Tio Pepe stood hospitably next to a portable radiogram. The walls reflected a catholic interest: cheap reproductions of Raphael, Renoir and Matisse jostled for space with rugger and cricket team photographs; over the mantlepiece hung a modern painting, large and presumably original, notable chiefly for a lurid splash of purple that looked as though it had been dropped on in error.

Barnaby studied the room with care, even casting his eyes momentarily through a copy of Orwell's *Selected Essays*. He had to admit he liked Begbie and found it hard to connect him with the murder. Common sense warned that there was no real reason for him to be excluded.

The next room was Maitland's and it, too, was empty. The first impression was of a facsimile of the room he had just left—another masterpiece of untidiness. But a longer glance disclosed a gulf between the characters of the occupants. Begbie's room suggested he had considered order as a desirable end in itself but had discarded it in favor of more important things. His was the disarray of a mind seeking higher aims—in whatever dilettante fashion—to the exclusion of trivialities. Maitland, on the other hand, seemed to have few cultural interests; his disorder was mere carelessness without any redeeming mental preoccupation. The books on the shelves were poor novels and his pictures had been chosen to fill space rather than to give aesthetic satisfaction. In one corner a gramophone had been left with its lid open and a record on the turntable. Barnaby turned it around to see the title. *The One You Adore*. Behind the door was a crate of empty beer bottles; in a wall cupboard was a miscellaneous supply of drinks—gin, whisky, vodka. . . .

"Good afternoon, Inspector. Looking for something?"

A characteristic remark, thought Barnaby, as he turned to face the owner of the room. He did not think it merited a reply. He said: "Just the man I want to see, Mr. Maitland. I'm sorry to trouble you again, but we've checked your account of Wednesday evening and nobody has yet corroborated your story. Would you care to reconsider it?"

"Certainly not, Inspector. If no one confirms my story, you must have asked the wrong people." He came in and shut the door.

"I don't think so, Mr. Maitland. We've been to the pubs you mentioned and none of the landlords saw you that evening."

Maitland flushed. "You're wrong, Inspector, or your henchmen are. I went to those pubs. If you think I went anywhere else, it's up to you to find out where. And before you ask any more damn fool questions, I suggest you get some evidence against me. What motive could I possibly have for wanting Carter out of the way?"

Barnaby watched him carefully. Maitland's behavior was following the pattern he might have predicted after their first meeting. He said: "I don't know yet. But if you haven't got one you're being remarkably foolish."

"I know what I'm doing." The reply was immediate and aggressive.

"I don't think you do." He moved toward the door. "You realize I shall have to talk to Miss Grant again? Think it over."

Aware that his last remark had been as weak as Maitland's, he hurried away. In his haste he failed to shut the door properly. Inevitably Maitland slammed it.

Barnaby's inspection of Warren's rooms revealed nothing new. It confirmed the impression of quiet efficiency he had gained already, conventional, perhaps, but ordered and masculine. The pictures were mostly photographs—the College XV and Boat Club, an informal shot of Warren's battery taken in a Normandy orchard shortly after D-Day, and numerous Claydon School teams. In one corner a pile of bats, pads and stumps did something to balance the austerity of the disciplined bookshelves. The colors were muted and the chairs leather; it had the air of a well-run gentleman's club. Only the typewriter interested Barnaby, and he typed out the anonymous message again before leaving.

He was intending to go to the matrons' rooms, but on the stairs he met Warren himself. There was a sense of concern about him Barnaby had not seen before.

"I'm glad I caught you, Inspector. I should like a private word. It's serious."

"Of course. Come up to the study."

Warren was silent until they got beyond the Big Door. As it closed behind them, he said: "I don't know what to make of it, but it could be dangerous. I've had three rounds of ammunition stolen."

"What on earth. . . ?"

"I know, 'What on earth did I have ammunition for?'"
Warren looked straight back at Barnaby, whose arm was
raised in expostulation. "I kept it after the war. It fits this."

He felt in a pocket beneath his gown and pulled out a
German Luger. "It's been gathering dust in a drawer for
years. But since Carter's death I've been checking it and
when I looked after lunch the ammunition had gone."

"Who knew you had it?"

"I'm not sure. I've shown Maitland and Begbie and I
think I've mentioned it to the others. Not Gregory, of
course—he's only just arrived."

Barnaby bent and peered at Warren. "Has anyone else
got a gun as far as you know?"

"Gregg's got a shotgun he uses on the pigeons, but
otherwise I don't think so. In any case, I think you'd better
take care of this for the time being. It's obviously not safe in
my room. It's not loaded." Frowning, he held out the gun.

Barnaby put it in his pocket thoughtfully. Somehow
Warren's uneasiness was as disturbing as the loss of the
ammunition. It was as if the whole affair had suddenly
acquired a new dimension.

CHAPTER TWENTY-TWO

SERGEANT GRAHAM was enjoying himself. His morning had been spent touring public houses and his afternoon was to be dedicated to two young women. More important, he was working on his own and not in the shadow of the tireless Barnaby.

He made his way to the kitchen, where he hoped to find Mary Croft, but it was her half-day and she had gone home at lunchtime. Eventually, after fending off innumerable leading questions from Mrs. Greaves, who like the boys, seemed not unwilling to pin the murder on Mrs. Quail, he discovered the girl's address and escaped from the steam of the washing-up into the open air. Outside he wiped his forehead and set off for the village. Yet despite the leisurely pace he adopted, he was perspiring freely again by the time he reached the white cottage on the Frome road where the Crofts lived.

The door was opened by Mary herself, a pretty girl whose pert and rather obvious charms were only marginally dimmed by having her hair wrapped in a towel.

"Washing my hair," she explained unnecessarily. "My

Mum's out, Sergeant. I expect she'd give you a piece of her mind if she was here. She's not very pleased at my being mixed up with the police. It's not respectable." She laughed and shook out her auburn hair over her shoulders.

Graham started by going over once again the times she had given for the serving of Carter's last meal and her own departure afterward. She remained consistent, so he edged toward new information.

"I expect you know a good deal of what goes on up at the school, don't you?"

"I suppose so. There's not much else to talk about in the kitchen. We see some things and guess others."

"And sometimes you hear things?"

"Sometimes." She was on her guard now.

"Have you heard anything which might have a connection with Carter's death?"

Her lips pursed and she appeared to be thinking. "No," she said firmly, almost as though trying to convince herself.

"Look, Miss Croft"—Graham spoke patiently—"I might as well tell you that we know you overheard an interview in Mr. Carter's study at the beginning of term. Miss Grant was with him, wasn't she?"

"Who told you?" She threw back her head in a manner which in other circumstances might have been coquettish.

"Never you mind, my dear. But you ought to realize that kitchen gossip doesn't stay secret for long. Now come on. Be sensible."

"All right—but I wasn't listening on purpose."

"Of course not."

"Well, I happened to be polishing the lino in the corridor outside the study when I heard Mr. Carter raising his voice. I'd never heard him angry before, so I was surprised. He sounded furious—almost out of control."

She stopped and stared hard at the gray rug in front of the fireplace.

"Go on. What did he say?"

"I don't remember the exact words, but it was something like this: 'If you go on seeing Maitland, and you know what I mean by that, you will both leave at the end of term, if not before. I'm not putting up with it in my school.'"

"Probably word perfect," thought Graham cynically. He suspected her ear had been very close to the keyhole indeed, and her fluency suggested she had told the story many times before.

She went on: "I knew Miss Grant was in with him, but I didn't hear what she said in reply. I didn't catch everything Carter said next either because he seemed to have calmed down, but it was something about writing to her grandmother and that it was the sort of thing that might kill her. Miss Grant came out after that, as white as a sheet, and looking very angry. I made myself scarce behind a cupboard in the corridor. I didn't want anyone to think I had been listening on purpose."

"And that was all you heard—nothing more?"

"No, that was all. And I was surprised, I can tell you. I didn't think he was capable of telling anybody off—everyone answered him back, you know, boys and all. He just didn't get any respect and he didn't seem to expect it. If there was a dirty job that needed doing, he would do it himself rather than ask someone else to. He was always pottering around, picking up paper, filling inkwells—he even emptied the dustbin once. I don't know—he somehow had no idea how a headmaster ought to behave. That's what I thought, anyway."

"Hardly a reason for murdering him though, is it?" said Graham. "Still that's very interesting. Now Miss Croft, to

go back to Wednesday night. When you came home, which
way did you come?"

"The usual way—the short cut across the fields and
through the woods. I only come by the drive and the lane
when it's been raining."

"That would take you near the swimming pool, wouldn't
it?"

"Yes, I did go past it. But I didn't see Mr. Carter there,
honestly I didn't." She was on the defensive again.

"Did you see anyone on the way home—anyone at all?"

"No—I don't think so. Yes, wait a minute, I did. I'd
forgotten all about it till now. Yes, I saw Mr. Jordon. He was
coming into the park through Gilley's Gate."

"Did he speak to you?"

"No, I don't think he saw me. He was walking with his
head bent—sort of concentrating. He's a funny man—
peculiar, you know. And now you come to mention it, I'd
never seen him in that part of the park before."

The village school was having its mid-afternoon break;
its forty-odd pupils cavorted and shouted in the small walled
playground. Standing in one corner presiding over the
disarray was Christine Bradby.

She was a pallid, bespectacled girl, with lank hair, the
type of plain Jane, thought Graham, who often becomes
friendly with a good-looker like Linda Grant. Surveying the
shrieking mob, she looked harassed.

Graham introduced himself, apologized for taking up her
time, and promised not to keep her long. She seemed
relieved to have her attention taken off the children.

"Miss Grant is an old friend of yours, Miss?"

"Yes, we were at school together in Taunton." Her voice
was soft—her greatest asset, Graham decided.

"What does Miss Grant think of the affair up at the school?"

"I think you should ask her that yourself, Sergeant."

The note of rebuke was reminiscent of Mrs. Quail. He ignored it.

"You were up at the Court on the evening of the murder, I believe, Miss Bradby? What time did you arrive?"

"I had tea with Linda at about four-thirty. I suppose I must have arrived ten minutes before that."

"Did she seem normal? She wasn't agitated at all?"

"No, not at all."

"And when did you leave?"

"Sometime between half-past seven and eight. We had supper before I came away. Linda walked down to the main gates with me."

"Were there any lights on in the school when you left?"

"No, I don't think so. No, definitely not. I looked up at it as I passed in the lane and there were no lights on then."

"And you saw nothing which could have any bearing on the case?"

"Nothing at all." She was almost flippant. "Mind you," she added with a sour smile, "I thought she was in a hurry to get rid of me—I suspected she was going to see Peter Maitland."

"Forgive my asking, Miss Bradby, but do you know anything of Miss Grant's relationship with Maitland?"

"Use your imagination, Sergeant." Her lips curled perceptibly.

"Like that, is it? What's Maitland like?"

"He wouldn't be my choice, but there's no accounting for taste. I wouldn't trust him far. Perhaps I shouldn't tell you this—I'm probably being disloyal to Linda—but his National Service in the army ended under some sort of a cloud. I'm not certain of the details but I think the I.R.A. got away with some rifles from an armory and it turned out that he'd been in bed with one of the NAAFI girls at the critical time. It was all hushed up, but he left the army early. If you ask me, it's her money he's after—Linda's due to get some useful pocket money one day, you know. But she's as blind as a bat where men are concerned. She's had them around her all her life but she still can't pick out a wrong 'un."

Graham ignored the ill-concealed bitterness coloring her voice. He was grateful it had loosened her tongue.

"How much," he asked, "is she going to get?"

She turned two pale blue eyes on him. "Why don't you ask her?" she said.

A hand-bell rang lustily inside the school and the shouting children drained away back to their classrooms. Graham and Christine Bradby were left like two fish stranded on the beach by the retreating tide.

CHAPTER TWENTY-THREE

THE study window was open but no breath stirred the curtains; the heat hung heavily, almost visibly, across the room. Outside, the afternoon was silent. The boys were still in the last period of school; Gregg, who had been mowing the front field all morning, had put his machine away, leaving the smell of cut grass behind him.

Barnaby leaned back in his chair, stretching his legs out straight under the desk. He closed his eyes and let the cast of characters in the case parade before him. One by one he mentally checked them off in best detective-fiction style. Begbie: No apparent motive; opportunity—yes. Warren: Motive—Yes, of a sort; opportunity limited. Maitland: Motive—

An authoritative knock on the door interrupted his reverie. He knew who it was: only one of his *dramatis personae* knocked like that. The door opened and Mrs. Quail came in.

"Inspector Barnaby," she said evenly, "I think I should tell you something."

Barnaby hauled himself to his feet and waved her into a

chair. She sat down with her usual confidence; as a concession to the heatwave she had discarded her tweeds and now wore a beige linen dress.

"You may remember, Inspector," she began, while Barnaby was once more adjusting his legs under the desk, "that when you asked me one of your questions last night I was abrupt in my reply. You asked if I'd heard any gossip about Mr. Maitland and Miss Grant. Perhaps you phrased your question a little awkwardly."

Barnaby made a sound at the back of his throat which might have been interpreted as acquiescence.

"Since then," she continued, "I have thought the matter over and I realize I may be hindering your investigation— that your inquiry was more than mere idle curiosity."

This time Barnaby nearly choked; his cadaverous face took on an unwonted shade of pink.

"The truth of the matter is that I've heard a good deal of talk, both from the boys, who are naive and frank, and in the village, where everything is seen in its worst light. Above all—and you understand that I speak in the strictest confidence—I've been on the spot to see for myself. Miss Grant is really only a foolish girl—she's only just twenty-one, you know. As a matron she's adequate as long as I keep an eye on her. Like most of her generation, she only does as much as she has to, and she's no idea at all how to handle boys. But she's learning and I don't want to seem too critical."

Barnaby, watching her over the tips of his fingers, said nothing. This was the type of narrative it was wise not to interrupt. But he was already toying with an idea which had formed since she entered the room.

She went purposefully on: "Whatever her qualities as a matron, however, Miss Grant is undountedly attractive to men." She lowered her eyes briefly before fixing them back on Barnaby, an action which said clearly, "As I'm sure you are aware." "I don't propose to say much about Mr. Matiland—I don't really know enough about him—but it's common knowledge that he has a reputation as a lady-killer and quite a number of people know that Miss Grant has fallen for him. Their relationship began to flourish—if that is the word—toward the end of last term and I've seen them together many times recently. I'm afraid, Inspector, that modern youth does not observe the proprieties as we did."

Barnaby winced. His ascetic nature resented the implication that he had ever been involved with such physical matters; his pride was hurt at being classed as a 'had been.'

"No, they do not observe the proprieties," she repeated. "I myself have seen them coming out of each other's rooms—often quite late at night. Probably innocent," she added charitably, "but not always politic."

"Miss Grant has never taken you into her confidence?"

"No, Inspector. I have never encouraged subordinates to entrust me with their secrets."

He thought this was to be the full extent of her revelations and felt disappointed she had not really told him anything he did not know already. But he was wrong.

Quietly and with an unusual diffidence, she said: "There is one other thing I should tell you, Inspector. You asked yesterday if I knew of Miss Grant's movements on the night of the murder. I said I knew nothing because her room is some way from mine. Now I certainly did not *see* her at all, but the stairs come up to the landing outside my room—as you will have noticed—and I'm sure that Miss Grant went out after I'd finished putting the boys to bed. I heard her on the stairs—I always know when she's going out. I expect she's told you where she went, but I thought I ought to tell you."

"What time was this?"

"Some time after 8:30. I'd only just reached my room
had hadn't even sat down."

This confirmed what Barnaby already suspected: Linda
Grant had lied. But he was still interested in Mrs. Quail.
"Why didn't you tell me last night?"

Her confession was over and she now reverted to her
normal style. "Because I suspected Miss Grant had gone
out with Mr. Maitland and I could not see that their private
relationship might have anything to do with the Headmaster's death. However, I've slept on it since then and I see
that although it is probably irrelevant I was wrong to keep it
to myself."

Mrs. Quail rose to go. She had imparted her information
and was now terminating the interview. Her quiet confidence and the way she took the initiative annoyed Barnaby.
Of all the personalities in the case, this was the one he could
not control. He decided to take a chance.

"One moment, Mrs. Quail," he said quietly.

She was already touching the door handle. Surprised, she
looked over her shoulder.

"Are you sure there's nothing else?" he said.

Puzzled, Mrs. Quail turned to face him. "No, Inspector. I
have omitted nothing this time."

He moved forward sharply, his lean frame rigid with
tension as he spoke: "What about that bombed house in
Kensington, Mrs. Quail?"

For a moment it looked as though the shaft had missed its
mark. There was no visible response beyond the flicker of
an eyelid; the masterly confidence remained untarnished.
Then, like some huge primitive animal which only slowly
realizes it has received its death wound, she began to
crumble. Her face was suddenly gray; those years which she
usually shrugged off with vigor and vitality crowded down

upon her and she looked old. She sat down carefully, her eyes lowered.

Barnaby was shocked. He had never seen a collapse as comprehensive and withering as this. Slowly, layer by layer, the protective shell of a powerful character peeled away; there before him, robbed of all strength, sat a feeble old woman. She even seemed to have shrunk in size.

"What do you want to know?" Her voice was a hoarse whisper, barely aubidly. He was surprised she still had the power of speech.

"I presume that you are Mrs. Lake?"

"Yes."

"Do you admit that you've been sending Mr. Carter anonymous notes with newspaper cuttings?"

"Yes."

"Where are your sons?"

"They do not concern us. One died over ten years go, the other is abroad."

"You are quite certain about that? Neither of them is by any chance teaching here in the school?"

"No." Her voice remained barren, reflecting a void.

He did not relent, though elation at his success had almost turned to pity.

"You realize, Mrs. Quail, that you have withheld information which may have a bearing on the case. You understand that I know the full story of your husband and that this now constitutes a possible motive for murder, particularly as you have seen fit to conceal the whole affair. Is there anything more you want to say?"

"It's got nothing to do with murder, Inspector. I was carrying on a private fued with Carter—you know why. And I hope he lived a few of those ghastly moments my husband went through beneath the ruins of our home. I didn't want to kill him—you must take my word for that—but I wanted him to share some of the horror and fear." Her voice was still tired, but there was a new edge to it, bitter and remorseless.

"But Carter didn't leave your husband to die on purpose," protested Barnaby involuntarily.

"I know. But there are times when incompetence is as culpable as crime: this was one of them. He was a hopeless failure at everything he attempted. That was why he infuriated everybody here, and it may even be the reason why somebody decided to kill him."

"When did you start sending your cuttings?"

"In 1948. I had stopped going to see my husband two years earlier. He was completely insane and didn't recognize me or our children. There was no point in going on. He was not the man I had married—the body was the same, but there was nothing inside. As I left that vacant face for the last time, I decided that Carter would have to pay—not enough, but something. I discovered he was teaching at a school in Herefordshire and started to send my notes. I can't expect you to image the pleasure I got when I thought I was worrying the life out of him."

Barnaby looked at her sharply; he did not interrupt.

"I sent him a note and a cutting once a year, on the anniversary of the bombing. How did you know it was me?" she ended abruptly.

"I didn't," he admitted. "I made a guess which happened to be accurate. Quail is very like Lake, isn't it?"

She inclined her head.

"And what was your reaction, Mrs. Quail—I think I shall continue to call you that—when you discovered Carter was coming to Claydon Court?"

"It was a coincidence up to a point, but not as strange as all that. There's a limited field for prep. school headships and he fell into the right age group, so it was quite likely he would apply. And when he did, I did all I could to get him here. I've been at Claydon a long time and I know one or two of the Governors. Her eyes narrowed. "I wanted to see him squirm when he got my notes. I wanted him here. . . ."

"And you enjoyed torturing him?"

"No. Oddly enough, when he'd been here a little while, I realized what a weak, insignificant man he was and there isn't much pleasure in crushing a fly. He worried about *everything*, and everything he touched went wrong. I soon despised him as much as I hated him."

"But you did not murder him?"

"No—I had nothing to do with it, and I've no idea who did."

In a curious way she was regaining her poise, though her voice remained quiet.

"Just one more thing, Mrs. Quail, and then you may go. What was the date the bomb fell on your home?"

"The twenty-third of May, 1941."

"I see. Today is the twenty-fifth. The twenty-third was Wednesday—the day Carter was killed."

CHAPTER TWENTY-FOUR

IMMEDIATELY after the last period of afternoon school, Warren collected the staff together. The problem that taxes all boarding schools at one time or another had raised itself in an acute form: What shall we do with the boys?

"I don't know what you all feel," he said, when they had once again gathered in the sticky heat of the staff room, "but it seems to me that we're entering a difficult stage. It's not so bad in the form room—though the boys have been keyed up all day—but there's going to be merry hell if we don't keep them occupied in their free time between now and bed. Listen—you can hear the din from here."

He stopped and, as if to underline his point, a minor stampede took place in the corridor outside. Judging from the shrieks, a small boy was being borne away to an obscure but painful fate.

"Any ideas, John?" asked Begbie.

"I don't think we have much choice, Mark. Swimming is obviously out, and cricket would occupy some but not all. We shall have to organize a hare-and-hounds chase. They can all take part—except anyone excused by Matron—

they'll be off the premises for a while, and if we take them far enough they'll be tired out at the end."

"Isn't it too hot?" objected Gregory, who tended to put the case of the unathletic boy.

"No, I don't think so. It's gone four o'clock and although it's still hot there's no reason why they shouldn't do a bit of running. Don't worry, Hugh, you needn't go," Warren ended with a laugh.

The chase was agreed; one small point remained—as they all realized.

"Well, who's going to be the hare?" agreed Begbie. For it was traditional at Claydon that whenever this particular form of exercise was decreed a master should run as hare. This guaranteed that the correct course was followed and that the quarry was not caught too soon; and, for some reason or other, the boys enjoyed chasing a master. Begbie suspected there could be only one answer to his question. Usually he or Warren did it, but today it was unlikely that Warren would be free. "I suppose I'm the mug," he said.

"I think so, Mark," replied Warren. "Unless anybody else feels like volunteering?"

Jordon made a vague puffing noise; Gregory shook his head.

Maitland said: "To old for that sort of thing. I swore I'd run my last cross-country when I left the army. You do it admirably, Mark. You're still young."

"All right. I'll get changed," said Begbie shortly. For once his good humor had deserted him. "What time do we start?"

"Four forty-five. Go and tell the boys, will you, Peter? Usual starting place—and make it clear there'll be trouble if anyone's late."

A short while later, the whole school had changed and assembled in a white gaggle in front of the cricket pavilion.

Begbie, now wearing a blue- and black-hooped rugger jersey and bearing a haversack of sawdust on his back, emerged from the pavilion. He received a high-pitched cheer. At the same time Warren and Maitland joined the group and the former gave final instructions to the hunt for the benefit of those who had not done it before. Eventually Begbie, running with long strides and accompanied by another cheer, set off down the drive. Five minutes later the pursuers were let loose and they streamed across the front fields to the main gates.

Begbie considered cross-country running an over-rated pastime. He excelled in any sport requiring skill with a ball, but running for its own sake had never appealed to him. Today it seemed more futile than usual. He was depressed. Something—he did not know what—told him that the tragedy being played out at the school was moving toward a climax.

He had already decided he would not allow himself to be caught. Usually a 'kill' was contrived at some point on the course, but the business of being brought home captive by innumerable small boys was inexpressibly tedious and he had no intention of submitting to it in his present mood. So he ran fast through the village and out on to the Frome road, leaving a large patch of sawdust every now and then to guide the pursuers. Just beyond the last cottage, he swung left down a track known obscurely as Pudding Lane and followed its dried-up ruts through the woods, then out into the open on Pendon Beacon. His pace slowed as the ground began to rise and by the time he reached the crest he was merely jogging.

In spite of his resolution to elude the boys, he paused for breath and to admire the view. Away on all sides stretched the rolling, irregular pattern of fields and woods, richly

green in the late afternoon sun. He pushed his hair back
with a characteristic gesture and said unexpectedly:

> *"And see the colored counties*
> *And hear the lark so high."*

"Hackneyed but evocative," he murmured. Housman
suited his mood. All those unfortunate rustics marching
away to death with the local yeomanry, or about to be
hanged for unnamed crimes in Shrewsbury Jail.

Hanging. Pendon Beacon had been used for that in the
past. How many poor devils, he wondered, had breathed
their last with that superb view before them to remind them
of the sweetness of life? And then dangled in chains for
months *pour encourager les autres*? What had Housman
called it? Keeping sheep by moonlight—yes, that was it.
But all that was over. Murderers didn't hang anymore.
Murderers. . . .

Drifting up from the valley beneath him came a faint cry:
"Tally Ho!" Looking down he saw the first runners break
the cover of the woods and begin to climb. They had spotted
Begbie on the skyline and thought the end of the chase was
near. He turned and sprinted for the trees on the other side of
the Beacon.

Barnaby watched the boys rushing off into the countryside with mixed feelings. It was a relief to be free from the
prying eyes of small boys, if only for a short while;
moreover, the peace that had fallen on the school was so
remarkable that, not for the first time, he found himself
rejoicing that he was neither a father nor a schoolmaster. On
the other hand, he felt the calm was deceptive, almost
ominous, and he reminded himself that the removal of the
boys might give someone else a chance too—someone who

had three rounds of ammunition and, presumably, the means and the will to use them.

He determined to pay Linda Grant another visit. He found her darning a pile of socks in the sewing-room, a tiny box overlooking the front fields. Sitting on a high stool, she displayed her figure to advantage.

"Do sit down, Inspector." She pushed forward a high stool similar to her own and smiled as he struggled to perch his gaunt frame on top of it.

"Miss Grant," he began, "I must ask you one or two more questions. I've had another word with Mr. Maitland."

"Yes?"

"When I first saw him yesterday, he told me he'd spent Wednesday evening in different public houses in the Mendips. But we've checked, Miss Grant, and no one remembers him."

"They must have forgotten. I'm sure if Mr. Maitland . . ."

"You don't really believe that, Miss Grant. It's much more likely that Mr. Maitland made a mistake. That's why I gave him a chance to—how shall I put it?—remember more accurately."

Barnaby tested her reactions by waiting. He was already convinced she knew more of Maitland's activities than she had admitted. Yet as he watched her he was puzzled. He detected conflicting emotions behind her cool façade. There was concern about concealment of the truth: that was understandable. But there was something else. Was it a suspicion that her deceit might not be justified?

She asked: "And what did he say?"

"Very little. But enough to convince me he lied last night. I wondered whether you might tell me the truth."

"Why did you wonder that?"

"Because, to be honest, Miss Grant, I'm not altogether

happy about the statement you gave me either. Are you sure you didn't forget anything?"

"Is this a trick, Inspector?" With studied care she uncrossed her legs, recrossed them, and adjusted her skirt.

The effect was lost on Barnaby. He leaned forward. "No, it is not. I believe you have lied. Where did you go on Wednesday evening?"

"I only went to the gates to see my friend off. I told you that."

"I mean later on, Miss Grant. I have evidence which suggests you went out again later."

"Then it must be worthless evidence, Inspector." This time she tilted her head in a gesture of defiance.

"I doubt it. Let me ask you something else. How much do you get in your grandmother's will?"

"About twenty thousand pounds—though I don't know how you've heard about that."

"Sergeant Graham has been working hard, Miss Grant, and people tend to be envious. How old is your grandmother?"

"Eighty-six."

"So you might hope to come into the money fairly soon. What did Carter threaten to do about that will?" He spoke with sudden sharpness.

"You do know a lot, don't you? I'd better tell you the whole story, then you won't get hold of the wrong end of the stick."

"A very good idea, Miss Grant."

"My parents died when I was young and I was brought up by my grandmother. She's rich, kind when she can have her own way, and puritanical. She got me this job at Claydon under the last Headmaster. He was an old friend of the family and promised to keep an eye on me as it was my first job. When Mr. Carter took over, my grandmother wrote to him and from then on he saw it as his duty to watch over me like an old hen. It was really quite funny."

"Go on."

"Well, it seems he began to get it into his head that Peter Maitland and I were 'carrying on.' That's the way he put it—isn't it quaint? Anyway at the beginning of term he threatened to sack us both. There you are—that's the lot."

"And the twenty thousand?"

"He said he'd tell my grandmother I'd been 'less than virtuous'—and I suppose that would have been the end of the cash. She's a narrow-minded old thing still living in the past."

"Maitland knew all this?"

"Yes." Her voice was soft now.

"Just one more question." He paused, then: "Has Maitland got a gun?"

Her eyes widened in bewilderment; her hand moved involuntarily to smooth her skirt. "A gun?" she repeated. "No—no, I don't think so. He's never shown me one. Of course, he was in the army, but I'm sure . . . I'm sure . . ."

Her voice trailed away reflecting complete confusion. She looked as though she had been introduced to a strange new world devoid of familiar landmarks.

Barnaby grunted, slipped carefully off the stool, and left the room.

Begbie began to feel more cheerful as he dropped his last sawdust mark and turned back into the park. He was tired and hot, but he had evaded his pursuers and was looking forward to a cool bath. The boys would be dispirited but he couldn't help that.

The park was deserted; the air seemed heavier than ever. Certain that he was well ahead of the leading boys, he made a leisurely progress toward the pavilion to get rid of the haversack.

Unaccountably his depression returned as he approached the little white building. Somehow the closed shutters, looking like hooded eyes, were lifeless. The door was half open and a ray of sunlight cut across the bare boards inside. He pushed it wide open with his foot, slipped the haversack off and went in.

Immediately he was aware of a figure in the deep shadow behind the door. It was silent and quite still.

Sharply he said: "Who's there?"

There was no reply. The figure moved, slowly, menacingly.

"Who on . . . ?"

A loud report filled the small room.

CHAPTER TWENTY-FIVE

THE weather was breaking. The three police officers sat in Carter's study and heard the first mutter of thunder drifting through the window.

"About time, too, if you ask me, sir." Graham wiped his face with a handkerchief. "My clothes are sticking to me all over."

"What about me in my uniform, Sergeant? I wouldn't mind being in a civvy suit." Beckett's voice was plaintive.

Barnaby paid no attention. Hands in pockets, shoulders hunched, he stood at the window and stared out at the hills. The sky was blue overhead and the haze blurred detail as he gazed across the trees of the park; but the air was ominously still and now the thunder had died away the only sound was the throb of a tractor somewhere beyond the Long Gallow Woods. An angry ridge of black cloud peered over the line of the Mendips.

"Yes, its going to break," he said, turning away from the window. "And I've a feeling we're about to break this case. One or two points are beginning to fall into place, I think. But something's missing and I can't see what it is."

Graham and Beckett said nothing; they could see he was thinking aloud.

Barnaby was about to continue his soliloquy when there came the sounds of a slamming door and running footsteps approaching down the corridor. Somebody knocked feverishly. It was a boy, very ordinary boy, distinguished only by the brightness of his eyes and the sense of excitement he carried with him.

"Sir—sir—sir—"

"Steady now, son. Take it slowly. What's up?" Sergeant Graham came into his own.

"It's Mr. Begbie, sir." He looked hopelessly from one to the other. "He's lying on the floor of the cricket pavilion. There's something wrong with him. I think he may be dead."

The boy's high-pitched voice was strangely calm as he spoke the last word. The silence that followed was broken by another roll of thunder.

"Begbie? Not *Begbie*?" Barnaby exclaimed.

The boy was adamant. "Mr. Begbie, sir. He's lying—"

"Come on." Barnaby waited for nothing more. With the boy beside him and Graham and Beckett at his heels, he moved for the door. Together they clattered down the stairs and emerged on to the terrace.

It had been stifling in the school, but outside the first warm gusts of wind stirred the air. Barnaby was conscious of them as he strode toward the pavilion. His mind was working furiously, trying to fit this new occurrence into the pattern of events. Suicide? Murder? Either would be awkward if his previous theories had been anywhere near the truth. He had to admit that Begbie had not come into his reckoning at all; now he could hardly be ignored.

But perhaps there was no truth in the story at all. He had learned a lot about boys during his short stay at Claydon and there was always the possibility the disturbing events of recent days had encouraged an over-sensitive boy to imagine a situation which did not in fact exist. Or he might have made the whole thing up out of sheer devilment.

He looked down at the white face bobbing along beside him as its owner's legs tried to keep up. Instinctively he knew the story was true.

They reached the pavilion. The boy stood back, pointing. The door was ajar and sticking out into a patch of sunlight was a gym shoe, twisted at a grotesque angle.

"Stay with the boy, Beckett," ordered Barnaby, and he went inside, followed by Graham.

It was dark in the pavilion as there were no windows, only shutters that were propped open on match-days. But there were plenty of cracks, and the light which cut across the dusty floor showed clearly that the boy was not lying. Begbie was dead.

He was on his back, one leg doubled under him, the other projecting into the doorway. His right arm, outstretched as though making a dramatic gesture, vanished under one of the benches lining the walls.

"Open the shutter, Graham. Be careful."

The sunlight flooded in. Barnaby knelt down by the body. He did not have to look far for the cause of death: a neat bullet hole above the right ear showed where life had fled. Begbie's face was peaceful; its lines suggested, if anything, faint surprise. His right hand, under the bench, gripped a revolver. Carefully, using a handkerchief, Barnaby prised it out of the limp fingers. It was a Service revolver and the empty cartridge was still in the breech; it seemed to be jammed. Then he realized why. It was a German cartridge, and even with his limited knowledge of firearms he knew that a gun designed for rimless ammunition would not eject a round with a rim on its base. Any lingering doubt he might have had that it was one of the bullets stolen from Warren disappeared.

"Poor devil," he muttered under his breath. Aloud he said: "I've been a bloody idiot, Sergeant."

He was angry now. And as his anger rose, he saw the pieces of the problem dropping into place before him. Where there had been confusion and disorder, a clear and logical pattern was unfolding. The concert, Gregory's search in the grass, the Levellers, the stolen ammunition, the Kensington Blitz tragedy—all moved into perspective. The important stood out in relief, the trivial faded into the background. Yes, he could see it all now. And what a fool he'd been! But there would be plenty of time for self-criticism later; in the meantime action was needed.

"Right." Barnaby swung round on his colleagues. "Beckett, you stay here and don't let anyone near the place. Graham, get on to Taunton. We'll want the full murder squad again. And you'd better get that doctor from the village. What's his name—Bunthorne? Oh, yes, and take the boy with you. I don't want anybody else to know about this for the time being."

He bent down to the boy. "What's your name?"

"Hobbs, sir."

"Now, listen to me, Hobbs. You're to stay with Sergeant Graham until you're told you can go. Is that clearly understood?" Turning to Graham, he added: "Keep him close to your coat-tails, Sergeant."

Graham and the boy set off at a quick trot toward the school and the telephone.

Barnaby made another rapid inspection of the body and the immediate surroundings; then he, too, returned to the school, leaving Beckett on guard.

The case was almost over. Begbie's death had produced a moment of revelation in which the truth crystallized, despite the fog of lies surrounding it. Now all he had to do was to find the evidence to prove the point. As he crossed the terrace, Barnaby's taste for melodrama was already planning a dénoument in which the murderer's guilt would be self-confessed.

There remained two tasks before the scene was set: the first, a telephone call to the B.B.C., was short and confirmed in every respect the theory he had formulated; the second was a visit to Warren to arrange a full meeting of the staff at a quarter to eight.

Warren was wholly agreeable. The only snag was that as Barnaby insisted that everyone, including the matrons, should be present, somebody had to be found to look after the boys. At length Warren decided, with some reluctance, to ask the Vicar to supervise them. He sometimes took Divinity periods at the school and although they usually dissolved into uproar within minutes, the Vicar remained unmoved and could be relied upon to face each meeting with the boys in a spirit of totally unjustified optimism. Warren was not enthusiastic, but there was little choice; the only possible alternative was a policeman and that, he feared, might be worse.

He was frankly curious about the proposed meeting. "You must have a special reason for wanting us all together again, Inspector?"

"I have, Mr. Warren. I shall be able to tell you who killed Carter."

Warren's eyebrows arched. "And you want us all there? If you know who did it, Inspector, would it not be simpler—and perhaps kinder—to make an arrest and leave the tongues to wag afterward?"

"I'm not feeling kind at the moment—I never do when I'm dealing with murderers. But I have my reasons. I'm not just a sadist." His tone was brittle, barely concealing his underlying tension. "Now, Mr. Warren, where can I get hold of a gramophone?"

This time Warren did not register surprise or any other emotion. He said: "Begbie's got one—and so has Jordon, I believe. Begbie's is nearer and easier to get hold of. I'm sure he'll lend it."

"Good," replied Barnaby. He could not look Warren in the face.

Barnaby remembered the gramophone in Begbie's room from his afternoon visit and he went up to fetch it. He had no doubt that the late owner would approve of the use for which it was intended.

The records he wanted were more difficult. Begbie's collection was large and eclectic but concentrated on rarities rather than the standard repertory. Thus there were several early Haydn symphonies and oddities like Berlioz's *Lelio*, but no *Leonora No. 3*; likewise, concertos by Telemann, Janacek and Shostakovitch, but none by Brahms.

This meant a telephone call to a record ship in Glastonbury. It was closed, but mention of Scotland Yard galvanized its owner into action and he promised to deliver the Beethoven overture and Brahms's Second Piano Concerto at Claydon within half an hour. The promise was fulfilled, though the man from the shop was apologetic about the concerto.

"Old recording, I'm afraid, sir. I've had it in stock a long time. There's not much demand for the classical stuff down here, and where there is, it's usually 'Gems from the Ballet' or something like that. Mr. Begbie and Mr. Jordon are different, of course. They get all their records from me. There aren't many cultured gentlemen like them down here, you know."

He was obviously keen to get into conversation; Barnaby was not encouraging. "Oh, yes?" he said.

The record dealer, a bird-like man with a twitching nose, was not put off. "What's the hurry with these records, then?"

Barnaby grunted characteristically. The man laughed. "Sorry!" he said. "I know—secrecy and all that. But this part of Somerset's been fair buzzing with this murder. We haven't had anything like it since Hilary Perkins was strangled by her husband behind a bonfire on Claydon Magna village green the night of the V.E. celebrations. Quite a do, that was. He'd just come back on leave from Germany and found his wife playing around with some bloke who'd avoided his call-up. A real sordid case when the details came out. The Sunday papers lapped it up."

Barnaby was irritated, but with the case so nearly completed, he managed a wan smile. Eventually he managed to shoo the little man away.

"Weather's changing. Look at that!" was his parting shot. He pointed westwards.

The black cloud Barnaby had noticed earlier as it edged over the hills now towered, bank upon bank, like a massive head in the sky.

CHAPTER TWENTY-SIX

"WHAT does he want this time, do you suppose?" Gregory spoke quietly to Maitland at the door of the staff room.

"More bloody questions, I expect. The wretched man's convinced it's one of us and he's going around in circles trying to prove it. I bet he hasn't even rung up the loony bin at Beauchamp Hayley to see if they've lost anybody lately. I've a good mind to do it for him."

"Have you seen all the police on the front field again this evening? Something's up—Barnaby's no fool."

They were the last to arrive and the desultory conversation which greeted them faded as they sat down. Everybody looked expectantly at the end of the room where Barnaby stood, arms folded and head bent, seemingly unaware that he was still very oppressive. As Barnaby began to speak, the thunder cloud moved over the edge of the sun.

"I'm sorry to trouble you again, ladies and gentlemen, but I'm sure you will bear with me when I say this will almost certain to be the last time I shall have to call you all together. You see, the case is more or less over; I just need a few details to help me tie up the ends and then my job is done."

He spoke informally, but the tension had already built up again. It was in harmony with the brooding storm outside.

He went on: "First of all I must confess to disappointment. I'm disappointed that throughout this case I have been hampered by lies from people who should have known better. Some of you have had private secrets, nothing to do with the murder, which you thought were best hidden from me. As a result, I've wasted a great deal of time and only within the last two hours have I realized the truth. Now you will understand that I may have no alternative but to reveal things about certain people that might have remained hidden if I had been taken into your full confidence right at the beginning.

"In a few moments I intend to reconstruct the hour during which your headmaster was killed and this will involve making a critical inspection of those stories you told me yesterday. It's just coming up to eight o'clock, so we shall be able to have our timings exactly right."

Barnaby looked carefully around the room as he waited for the last minutes before eight to pass. Mrs. Quail, sitting between Linda Grant and Warren, seemed to have shrunk in size; she gazed fixedly out of the window at the broad sweep of the park. Linda Grant, pale and tense, was trying to catch Maitland's eye, but he, affecting an air of nonchalance, was lighting a cigarette; his hand was steady. Jordan was composed: he gave the impression of having come to terms with himself and the world at last; he looked, thought Barnaby, resigned. Warren was calm but making little attempt to conceal his ill temper; the taut lines of his face showed what he thought of policemen in general and this one in particular; the quicker the whole thing was over and he could get back to the business of running the school, the better. Gregory was obviously worried: his face was expressionless and his legs were crossed carelessly, but the knuckles of his hands were white as he gripped the arms of the chair and there were beads of moisture on his forehead.

Maitland was looking at faces, too. He burst out: "I say, where's Mark?"

"Mr. Begbie will not be coming," was the curt reply.

"Why not? Why should he be excused?" This time it was Gregory who spoke. "Do you mean you've let him off because he used some of his precious charm?" His lip curled and there was an hysterical edge to his voice.

"Don't be absurd, Gregory," intervened Warren before the inspector could answer. "Get that chip off your shoulder about Mark's class, for goodness' sake." He turned to Barnaby. "Is there a special reason why Begbie has been excused?"

An unusual flush had appeared on Barnaby's high cheek bones.

"For the present it is sufficient to say that he's not coming. He will not be able to help in what I propose to do."

"Good Lord!" exclaimed Jordon. "You've arrested him. You must be mad if you think he did it. Mark Begbie couldn't hurt. . . ."

"Be quiet, Mr. Jordon, please. You really must stop jumping to conclusions. Now"—he drew himself up to his full height—"please pay attention, all of you." He was in command, brisk and imperative.

A rumble of thunder, less distant than before, reverberated around the hills.

"The hour which concerns us is the hour between eight and nine. I have evidence sufficient to convince me that Mr. Carter was murdered during that time. I intend to reconstruct that hour for each of you here, piecing together your own accounts and the information I've acquired from other sources. To act as time-keeper, I shall use the music played in the B.B.C. concert which ran from eight to nine o'clock; one or two of you were listening to it. You will see that I have borrowed Mr. Begbie's gramophone and I've got hold of the right records."

"A bit sensational, isn't it?" said Maitland. "I mean, is all this music nonsense really necessary? We're not children, you know." He flicked his cigarette ash accurately toward the large tin that acted as a waste-paper basket.

"At times during this investigation, Mr. Maitland, the boys have shown more good sense than some of their mentors—but let that pass. I admit to a certain theatricality, but I have more pressing reasons as well." He looked at his watch. "It's time to begin, ladies and gentlemen."

He took out the record of *Leonora No 3* and put it on the turntable. He allowed the quiet opening bars to play before he went on.

"So it is eight o'clock. Where is everybody? Mr. Warren had just had his supper and is going to his study. For the time being we can leave him there, marking exercise books."

Warren nodded confirmation.

"What about Mr. Gregory? He is sitting in the lounge bar of the De Mallet Arms. And he's not the only one in the pub. Mr. Jordon is in the public bar, having an argument with someone, I believe. Both of these are confirmed by the landlord. By the way, Mr. Jordon, what were you getting so heated about?"

"I had a difference of opinion about wildcat strikes with a man called Palmer. He's a local troublemaker among the farm laborers here. I just tried to point out that unofficial strikes make the trade unions look ridiculous. I'd had too much to drink—it was my fault we ended up having a row."

Jordon blinked sadly; everyone else looked embarrassed.

Barnaby continued: "That leaves the two ladies and Begbie to be accounted for. At eight o'clock you, Mrs. Quail, were busy putting the boys to bed, and you, Miss Grant, enjoying your half-day, had just walked back to the school after seeing Miss Bradby down to the gate. The boys assure me Mrs. Quail was doing as she said and Gregg confirms Miss Grant's actions. Mr. Begbie claims he was devoting his evening to the concert"—at this point the overture climbed to a crescendo; Barnaby broke off to turn down the volume—"and I've no reason to doubt he was telling the truth."

Barnaby put down the notebook he had been using. "At that point, however, fiction began to take the place of truth and I've had to contend with a smokescreen of lies. Mr. Maitland, for example. You have told me a cock-and-bull story about visiting pubs in local villages. But not one single person will corroborate this. On the other hand, Gregg thinks he saw you in the trees near the swimming pool at about eight-thirty—a quarter of an hour after the time you claim to have left by car."

The mention of the swimming pool caused a stir; it was as if they had all drawn breath together.

Maitland said: "If you take any notice of that old fool Gregg, Inspector, you might as well give up the case. You know, of course, he's absolutely gaga. He's practically living in the nineteenth century. He couldn't tell the difference—" He stopped and laughed loudly.

"You are mistaken. Gregg may be old and he may not be an ideal witness, but he's nobody's fool. Working out there on the cricket square, forgotten by everybody as if he were part of the scenery, he saw more than most of you suspected. Besides, he wasn't the only one who saw you near the swimming pool, was he? What about Mr. Jordon?

But we're running ahead of ourselves. We must wait for the music to catch up."

The overture came to its triumphant conclusion. Barnaby took it off and replaced it with the Brahms concerto. "The time is approximately a quarter past eight," he said.

The haunting opening horn phrase was greeted by the first large drops of rain on the window and it was suddenly very dark.

Warren reached up and turned on the light. "It's going to be a snorter," he said. "I'm sorry for the poor Vicar looking after the boys in this. Some think thunderstorms a huge lark, others are terrified."

"So," continued Barnaby, "between 8:15 and 8:30 I know where you all are, except for Mr. Maitland, who still declines to face the facts. But as we get near to 8:30 several people begin to move. You, Mr. Jordon, left the pub and set off home by a roundabout route. Mr. Gregory, you also came back to the school. You're both confirmed by the landlord, Rugg, and old Granny Thatcher in the cottage opposite. And it was Jordon, coming into the park by the track from Gilley's Gate, who saw Maitland in the vicinity of the pool. And you saw Jordon, too, didn't you, Mr. Maitland? He was a good fifty yards away and you hoped his eyesight was so poor he hadn't recognized you. But he knew you all right—so perhaps you see why I'm so skeptical about your pub crawl."

Maitland shrugged; Jordon looked abstracted.

"But someone else was moving too. Miss Grant, you said you didn't go out again after getting back to the school, but Mrs. Quail is certain she heard you go out around about 8:30. And you yourself mentioned a light in Begbie's room—a light which was not there at 8 o'clock but which probably would have been soon after 8:30. I wonder, Miss

Grant, whether you went out for an assignation with
Maitland, perhaps not far from the pool?"

"Assignation," muttered Maitland. "You sound like
Carter."

Linda Grant placed her feet neatly together in front of her
and looked down at them. Barnaby stared at her; the others
eyed her obliquely.

"But then," went on Barnaby, ignoring her silence, "we
also have Mr. Jordon in the critical area and as I now know
he was a bitter man with a possible motive for murder, not to
mention the Dutch courage that might be required to
commit it."

Jordon immediately became the center of uncomprehending attention. He sat forward in his chair, spectacles tilted,
his face white in the artificial light.

"Yes, I had the motive all right," he said malevolently.

The first flash of lightning illuminated the park, closely
followed by a long roll of thunder. For a moment the
landscape was frozen by the glare, then the darkness
returned more complete than before. Only the pale blue
strip of sky fast vanishing in the east showed that the day
had been fine.

"For ten years I've taught at this wretched school, an
insignificant cog in an insignificant machine; for ten years
I've put up with the taunts of silly little boys who need
nothing so much as a good hiding. And all the while I've
gone back to the sanctuary of my work, my own real work,
despising the idiot boys and some of my colleagues who
seem to find me amusing. One day, I told myself, one
day. . . . And one day I'm told it's all wasted, useless, so
much rubbish. And who by? By Carter, the man who
allowed himself the luxury of a conscience without regard
to the consequences, the man who destroyed the last shreds

of discipline remaining in my form room. Yes, I had a motive."

He sat back in his chair shaking his head; his composure had gone, he was near to tears. Another flash of lightning and an immediate cascade of thunder swamped his last words. As it died away, the Brahms concerto came back into perspective, the piano sounding rough and metallic on the cheap machine.

Barnaby was speaking again: "Let's go back to Mr. Gregory. You left the pub shortly after Jordon and came back to the school via the main gates. At first you gave me the impression that you came straight up the drive, but this morning when I found you searching for . . . for a nest . . . you told me you'd left the drive and turned into the park. Not very consistent. Just think about it while Brahms catches up with us."

The energetic first movement ended and the scherzo began. Gregory said nothing.

"Yes, Mr. Gregory reached the main gates and started up the drive. I think we have the truth so far. But then you saw something, Mr. Gregory, didn't you? Something you couldn't resist, something you can never resist. You left the drive and walked along the edge of the Long Gallow Woods, across the fields where I found you this morning. This is what you were looking for, isn't it?"

Barnaby held up the small black knob.

Gregory seemed about to say something, then thought better of it and turned his head away.

"Not a bird's nest, Mr. Gregory. And I know where it comes from. But I'll leave you to your conscience for the moment. What were the rest of you doing? At about 8:30 Mrs. Quail went to her room after seeing the boys to bed. Mr. Begbie was still listening to the concert. They have no proof, but there's no reason to doubt them at the moment.

Mr. Warren was safely marking and he has some cover, more than the other two: at about 8:40 he had a telephone call from Browning's father, a call confirmed by the G.P.O. . . .

"But now we're coming to the crucial time and I must move ahead of the music. At about 8:35 Mary Croft served Carter's supper and at approximately 8:45 Gregg saw the Headmaster walking down to the pool.

"Then, at about three minutes to nine, Gregg saw someone running away from the pool toward the school. Whoever it was kept to the fringe of the trees and moved fast. He's positive it wasn't Carter himself, but it was too dark for him to see who it was. There's little doubt in my mind that that person is the murderer. Between a quarter to nine and nine o'clock Carter died. And one of you killed him."

CHAPTER TWENTY-SEVEN

THE concentration in the room did not waver as lightning flashed repeatedly and thunder rolled round the hills. It was raining hard now, threshing down in steel-colored rods. Barnaby turned the record and the third movement started.

He faced his audience again. "Now it is plain that a number of you could have been at the place of the murder at the critical time. To clear the ground, let's see if anyone could not have been there. What of Begbie? He was listening to the concert, but has no proof of it except that he claims to have heard the soloist collapse at the end. Anyway, he admits that Warren mentioned the incident when he went into Begbie's room shortly after 9:00. So Begbie is doubtful, but Warren seems to be on safer ground because if he definitely heard the collapse somewhere between 8:55 and 9:00 he could hardly have been down at the pool. As for Mrs. Quail, she claims to have been watching television, but there is no evidence that she was; on the other hand, her room is at the end of the building farthest away from the pool and she would have had to move very fast indeed in following Carter down if she was the unknown figure seen by Gregg on the way back."

"Nevertheless, I'm still a suspect," interrupted Mrs. Quail unexpectedly.

"You forget, Mrs. Quail, that I said I know who murdered Carter. Besides, your own behavior hardly qualifies you for exemption at this stage."

Barnaby dominated the room so completely that there were no signs of surprise that Mrs. Quail, the most powerful force in the school, had apparently been caught transgressing by this gaunt policeman.

"That leaves four of you outside," went on Barnaby. "Jordon and Maitland saw each other within a stone's throw of the pool, and Miss Grant could have been anywhere at all. Gregory, on his own admission, was moving in the right direction, but he was on the far side of the park and Gregg saw nothing of him. That is not conclusive, of course—Gregg missed several movements in the course of the evening—but Gregory was farthest from the pool and unless he had a previous arrangement with Carter, would have had no means of knowing the Head was there at all. That does not apply to anyone else. Those in the school could have seen him from the window and the others may have been near enough to see him arrive. Of course, it is possible that Gregory *did* have an appointment with Carter, but I have nothing to suggest it.

"So there you all are. Now we must wait for the one piece of evidence I need. Brahms is still in his third movement. Let's listen to some music."

The music was quiet and had difficulty in competing with the storm. Thunder boomed almost continuously and the rain was so straight that it no longer touched the windows. The ground, baked by a month's drought, could not absorb it and large puddles were forming. The whole park hissed and seethed with a life of its own. It was perceptibly cooler.

Jordon drew out his handkerchief and dabbed at his forehead. Gregory blinked. Warren looked severely at Linda Grant. None of them seemed to know what they were waiting for and puzzled curiosity almost edged out fear.

Barnaby began to fidget. He did not know this particular piece of Brahms at all, but he sensed the movement drawing to an end. Tense and expectant, he hovered over the gramophone. At length the music died away. Abruptly he turned off the machine and wheeled around.

"Well, ladies and gentlemen, that was where the pianist collapsed. Please look at your watches. What is the time?"

"About a minute after a quarter to nine," answered Maitland. "But what this hocus-pocus has to do with Carter's death I can't imagine. Really, Inspector, this is all very tedious. Do we have to—?"

Barnaby cut in sharply: "Exactly. A quarter to nine. The pianist collapsed at a quarter to nine!"—he repeated the last words triumphantly, his eyes probing the room—"At a quarter to nine!"

Then things happened swiftly. Although prepared for action, Barnaby was nearly taken by surprise. A jagged fork of lightning darted out of the sky and for an instant seemed to hang across the room itself. Momentarily, Barnaby had the impression that the figures before him had been transformed into carved stone images doomed to sit immobile for the rest of eternity. Even as the thread of purple light scorched the air, a rending crack of thunder pealed overhead.

Linda Grant, broken by the sheer physical impact of the storm, stood up, screamed, and threw herself into Maitland's arms.

A hand touched the light-switch; the room became

suddenly dark. There was total confusion. A chair over-
turned; somebody swore fearfully; Linda Grant screamed
again.

Barnaby bellowed: "Watch out, Graham!"

The door was open now and the general frenzy resolved
itself into an individual commotion in the corridor outside.
Barnaby reached the light-switch.

Graham was getting to his feet in the corridor. He was
flushed and disheveled; his hat had come off. "Lost him, sir.
Too strong for me. You wouldn't think to look at him—"

Barnaby cursed and pushed past him. "Come on, man.
He won't get far."

The corridor, high and narrow, ran the length of the
building. At the far end, making for the glass-paneled door,
was John Warren.

He reached it a good twenty yards ahead of his pursuers,
stopped for an instant to lock it behind him, and ran out into
the rain.

"Front door!" shouted Barnaby above the thunder, and
they turned left down the passage that led to the main
entrance. Within seconds they too were out in the rain.

At first the storm was so overwhelming that Barnaby was
aware of nothing but its noise. Then he saw the white
ambulance and the police car by the pavilion and a small
knot of uniformed figures huddling near the door. And just
beyond the pavilion, heading for the woods, was Warren.

Barnaby and Graham stopped at the pavilion and the
former shouted to the policemen sheltering under the
dripping shutters. "Gilley's Gate! He's heading for Gilley's
Gate. Take the car, one of you, and cut him off in the
village. The rest of you, follow me."

Across the cricket field and past the uncomprehending
cows in the meadows beyond, Barnaby, Graham, and three
constables chased Warren, who now had a lead of more than

a hundred yards. Reaching the track to Gilley's Gate, Warren crossed it and plunged into the dense woodland beyond.

"Where the devil's he going?" muttered Barnaby. Then he realized and shouted to Graham at his elbow: "The old railway—he's making for the cutting."

When they reached the trees, there was some protection from the rain, though it still managed to get through and the tangled undergrowth was sodden. Barnaby remembered the rough direction of the cutting and took the lead. Ahead, Warren had disappeared; behind, he heard the noisy progress of his colleagues.

At length he emerged above the cutting, roughly where he had come out previously. To a young constable who was now leading the rest of the field he grunted: "There he is. Down on the old line."

"It's the viaduct that way, sir, and the Claydon Hill tunnel at the other end."

Clutching at bushes and bracken, they scrambled down the slope and reached the level of the old track. Warren was already out of sight beyond the curve of the cutting. They ran to the bend, expecting to see him halfway across the viaduct. But when they reached the corner and had a clear view to the tunnel on the other side of the valley there was no sign of him. The viaduct, gray and bleak in the lashing rain, was deserted.

The logic of the situation allowed but one answer. Barnaby ran forward, splashing through puddles and slipping on the stones in which the sleepers had once been set; near the middle of the viaduct he pulled himself up on to the stonework of the parapet and looked over.

At the far end of the valley, just visible through the curtain of rain, a train from London curled around the base of Clayton Hill. Immediately beneath him, in a field by the main line, crumpled and strangely twisted, lay the inert form of John Warren.

"Broken neck—instantaneous." Barnaby moved his hand in a characteristic gesture.

His audience—Graham, Beckett, and Inspector Single-ton—who had gathered in a private room at the De Mallet Arms, did not interrupt.

"I was bluffing a bit when I told them I knew who had killed Carter. I had a shrewd suspicion but no proof. You see, I knew what some of them had been doing and the rest followed by a process of elimination.

"Take Maitland and Grant, for instance. It didn't need a genius to guess they had been together at the critical time. He was waiting for her near the pool when Jordon saw him. And if they were together, one could surmise what they had been doing."

"You London people," laughed Singleton, "you always jump to one conclusion."

"Just human nature. But if they were together, it wasn't likely they had anything to do with Carter's death."

"Why did they lie?" asked Graham. "Just because they didn't want anyone to know they were carrying on?"

"Partly. But don't forget that they had the most obvious motive of the lot. Twenty thousand pounds is a good deal of money to lose overnight. In other circumstances they would have been top of my suspect list, but I couldn't take Maitland seriously as a murderer. He's a stupid man in many ways, but he could hardly have hoped to get away with his story if he wanted to hide anything really important. No, they'd been enjoying themselves in the long grass, and it was Maitland, of course, whom Mrs. Quail saw going to bed when she was coping with the boy who had been sick."

"That knocks out two of them. What about Gregory?" asked Singleton.

"Yes, I admit he confused me. When I found him crawling about down by the woods, I thought I'd gone back to square one. And I couldn't for the life of me think what the black knob was. But then I remembered something Granny Thatcher said. She spoke about seeing Gregory looking in one of the local barns. She assumed he was keeping an eye on one of the rivals for the favor of a village girl, but I saw another possibility—not at the time but later. Gregory is a *voyeur*—a Peeping Tom. Nothing more, nothing less. And that explained how he fitted into the scheme of things on the night of the murder. One of the patches of beaten grass I found was where he had been lying; the other, the one in the hollow, was the scene of the Maitland-Grant escapade. He must have spotted them on his way back from the pub. He knew the sort of terms they were on, so he guessed what was up. All he had to do was wait until they had settled down for a long session then he found a good vantage point for his own vicarious enjoyment."

"And the black knob?" said Graham.

"Off his binoculars. He always had them with him, whether for birds or for his own more private pleasures." He sat back looking pleased.

"Did you confront him with it?" asked Singleton. "It's hardly the sort of thing he'd admit, is it?"

"No, but he knows I know all about him. I watched his eyes during my little performance this evening. He was terrified I was going to expose him. And I would have done, too, if things had gone wrong. He'd wasted too much of my time to get any sympathy from me. Anyway, the Peeping Tom is not a breed I encourage."

"Some of them are sad cases," said Singleton. "We've

had a number down here recently. I don't think they can help it."

"I don't agree," grunted Barnaby. "I was brought up to value the virtue of self-control, in the days when crime was called crime and not some sort of psychological disease."

"When did you rule Jordon out?" interposed Graham tactfully.

"I didn't. He was always a possible. He was in the right place and he had the motive. But he didn't strike me as a murderer—that's feeble, I know—and I think he was too drunk for it anyway. Nor did I think he could run as fast as the person I chased last night.

"That didn't go for Mrs. Quail, incidentally. I think she could move if she wanted to. But I had strong reservations about her, too. She's tough, she had the motive, and she was clever enough to fool me with trousers in the bonfire. But when I confronted her with the anonymous letters, she broke down completely. I've never seen a soul so pitifully naked. If she had killed Carter, I think she would have admitted it there and then. As it was she denied it, and I believed her."

"So the field was thinning out."

"Yes—but it was my unexpected visit to the staff room during break this morning which gave me what I wanted. That, and Begbie's death. I barged in while they were discussing the case among themselves. Begbie was explaining what he was doing on the night of the murder and, quite by chance, I heard the important bit."

"Do you mean he didn't tell us the truth, sir?" asked Graham.

"Oh no. He told the truth, all right. It was just that he added a detail we hadn't picked up. Do you remember what he said about the time before Warren joined him?"

Graham produced his notebook. "Yes, here we are. He

said he was listening to the concert until the girl playing the piano collapsed. Then there was a lot of stuff about the music being too difficult for her—I didn't put it all down."

"And then?"

"Then the talk started at nine and Warren arrived immediately afterward."

"You've missed something, Sergeant," said Barnaby complacently. "And so did I until I heard Begbie say it for a second time this morning. He said there was a fill-in before the talk that began at nine: that's what we missed. And I'd have missed it again if he hadn't added something. This time he said what the fill-in was."

"And what was it?" asked Singleton.

"Handel's *Water Music*. I saw straightaway that I'd jumped to an unjustifiable conclusion—and so had Warren. We had both assumed that because the pianist reached the end of the third movement she had finished the concerto—to my limited musical knowledge, concertos have three movements. But she hadn't, you see. The Brahms B flat, as I learned this afternoon, is an oddity that has *four*. We should have listened more carefully to poor Begbie when he bumbled on about it being too hard, too strenuous and so on. Part of its difficulty is its sheer length."

"But how did the *Water Music* help?"

"Pure luck. I've always had a soft spot for Handel and I happen to know this piece. Now when Begbie mentioned a fill-in between the concerto and the talk, I imagined a two- or three-minute record—you know the sort of thing. But the moment he said they played the *Water Music*, I knew it must have lasted much longer. The Harty arrangement is nearly a quarter of an hour's work—actually about fourteen minutes, as I discovered when I rang the B.B.C. earlier this evening."

"But why did Warren kill Begbie, sir?" asked Beckett, speaking for the first time.

"Because when Begbie mentioned the Handel, Warren realized he had made a mistake, too. You see, on the night of the murder he thought the Brahms had finished at the end of three movements, just as I did. He'd seen Carter go down to the pool and when he heard the girl collapse it suddenly occurred to him that this would make a rough sort of alibi. On the spur of the moment he threw on a pair of gym shoes, dropped in at the staff room to pick up the knife from the confiscation box, and sprinted down to the pool. Remembering that Gregg was on the cricket square, he took a roundabout route, using the trees at the back of the school as cover. On the way back he must have been nervous, or else time was short—anyway he ran direct and Gregg saw him. Then he dropped in on Begbie and made sure that he mentioned the pianist's collapse first."

"But what about the missing time?" interrupted Singleton. "He must have realized it would have to be explained."

"Yes, he did. But you must remember that this was not a premeditated murder, not in the planning sense anyway. Warren's hatred had been building up a long time, but when he eventually took action it was suddenly, in a flash of anger. So he took a big risk, as any impulsive murderer does. But luck was with him and has been right through the case except for this evening. He guessed that Begbie would listen to the talk which followed the concert and he was right. But his real stroke of luck came on the times he was playing with. Imagining that the collapse had been at a few minutes to nine and that he would have to account for the quarter of an hour following, he assumed he would have to convince Begbie that he had arrived shortly after the beginning of the talk so that the time lag would not have been long enough for him to have been down to the pool. But Begbie did not need any convincing because he *had* come in just a minute or two after the hour, just as the talk started. With the collapse of the girl round about 8:45, fifteen minutes earlier than he thought, Warren was trying to account for the wrong period of time."

"That still doesn't explain why he killed him. Surely Begbie was his salvation if you got too near the truth?"

"Yes, he was in a dilemma all right. But the moment he knew he'd missed the *Water Music*, he saw Begbie was dangerous. He guessed Begbie had told me about the fill-in whereas he hadn't mentioned it. In fact, I missed the discrepancy altogether."

"Did you know immediately that Begbie hadn't killed himself, sir," asked Graham.

"Oh yes. If he had shot himself it would have been difficult for the bullet to have entered his head at that angle. And there was the gun. The way he had fallen with his arm under the bench it would almost certainly have been knocked out of his hand if he had shot himself. As it was, he was holding it very carefully indeed. Besides, the whole gun business was suspicious. I felt something wrong when Warren told me the ammunition was stolen and handed in his gun. He seemed genuinely worried for the first time—in a way that was out of character. At the time I put it down to understandable concern, but later I saw it could all be a blind and that he might have another gun. And once Begbie was shot, it all pointed to him. Apart from Maitland, who could still not be ruled out, he was the only one who might be expected to know that German and English rounds are interchangeable."

Barnaby's mood changed. The air of complacency gave way to depression. "No, there's no doubt about it: I made a mess of this one. I ought to have foreseen an attempt on

Begbie. There's really no excuse for his death at all. He was the one person in the whole affair who had nothing to reproach himself with—and now he's dead."

He stood up abruptly, the joints of his body moving in their inevitable way. "If he hadn't killed Begbie, I would have had some sympathy for Warren. Carter's murder was a matter of principle in an odd sort of way. I think he felt it better that one man should die than that the school should be destroyed. But killing Begbie was just a selfish attempt to save his own skin. Knowing he had done that, I must confess that I enjoyed watching him squirm this evening. He was suspicious right at the beginning, but he wasn't *certain* I knew and he didn't dare to make a bolt for it until I made the point about the missing fourth movement. Then he was away, and the storm gave us a positively Wagnerian climax."

"Astonishing that a man can feel like that about a school," said Singleton.

"It's not as simple as that," replied Barnaby. "I've talked with several members of the staff this evening when they'd all relaxed and I think I begin to understand him now. You see, Warren was a belated victim of the war. Outwardly, he was the most balanced man in the place, inwardly he was twisted. War upsets the moral code. 'Thou shalt not kill' becomes 'Thou shalt kill, and go on killing, if the cause is just.' This is all right in war—a pacifist, of course, would say it isn't—but it creates problems when peace returns. Once the absolute commandment has been qualified so that black has become white, it's not surprising a few men find it hard to get back to normal. Warren never made the adjustment. He had an exemplary war record—I've checked on that—and when it was all over he gave the same dedicated service to the school that he'd given to fighting Nazi Germany. When the school was threatened by Carter's incompetence, his unbalanced mind could provide only one solution. The just cause needed action. . . ."

"Thought you disapproved of all the psychological stuff," said Singleton, smiling.

"So I do when it's made an excuse for people who are as aware of right and wrong as you or I. But Warren had lost his moral bearings. In certain circumstances, and this was one of them, wrong could become right. I very much doubt if he had any sense of guilt at all."

Barnaby stretched his arms above his head and yawned massively. "Bed," he said. "But now it's my turn to ask a question." There was a sly gleam in his eye. "How did the Vicar get on?"

"Another failure, sir," said Graham. "He gave the boys a talk on prisons—he's a prison visitor, I gather—got carried away describing solitary confinement, and ended up being locked in a broom cupboard. I don't think he'll ever learn."

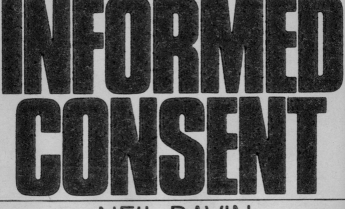